ABOUT THIS BOOK

More than anything, Clarke Price hates the cold, so when she and her mom pick up in the middle of winter to move to the small town of Havenwood Falls in the Rocky Mountains, she is less than thrilled. On the way to their new home, their car hits a patch of black ice, sending them into a ditch. When Clarke wakes up, she finds herself stuck with an aunt she's never met, while her mom recovers in the hospital. She's never felt so alone.

While Clarke grapples with impossible truths about the town, her family, and the unbelievable realization that she's a witch, she keeps running into a stunning guy with gorgeous eyes who turns her into her least favorite cliché. He's rude, always around, and has a knack for bringing out her argumentative side. But even that isn't enough to dampen her growing attraction to him.

But can Clarke trust this handsome stranger, or is he responsible for the accidents that have nearly taken her life—twice? And what about the nightmares that feel like a dire warning that something bad is coming?

More than just her life rests on Clarke finding the truth in time.

CAST IN MOONLIGHT

A HAVENWOOD FALLS HIGH NOVELLA

ALI WINTERS

HAVENWOOD FALLS HIGH BOOKS

Stay up to date at www.HavenwoodFalls.com

ALSO BY ALI WINTERS

THE HUNTED SERIES

The Reapers

The Exodus

The Moirai

The Fallen

Flirting with Death

Sound of Silence

A Sky of Shattered Stars

Army of the Winter Court

Favor of the Gods

For Michelle Fritz,
Your friendship is worth more than
all the books in the world.

CHAPTER 1

I crack open my eyes and instantly regret it. Bright florescent lights flicker above, accompanied by the harsh glare of sunlight through the window, and an annoying, constant beep. I squeeze my eyes shut before I can focus on anything and groan, trying to roll over. I can't. It hurts too much. Every inch of my body aches, and I think every part of me must be bruised.

Voices murmur nearby. I can't make out what they're saying. One belongs to a man, the other to a woman. I don't know who they are. The talking stops as I reach up to place a hand over my splitting head.

There's a tug on my hand, and I realize I'm attached to something.
What happened? Where am I?

I force my eyes open again. White walls, a soft blue knitted blanket draped over my legs, and a railing on either side of my bed. I'm in the hospital, or at least something like one. The room is small. There's not really much to it.

Before I can fully get my bearings, a woman approaches. The one who must have been talking to the man in a white coat just outside the door.

"Oh good, Clarke, you're awake," she says.

It takes me a moment, but I recognize her from pictures Mom

showed me years ago. The two of them on a road trip in the nineties, the summer before college, taking selfies before it was even a thing.

Looking at her face is like looking into a mirror where I've aged, though only slightly, perhaps only by a few years. But unlike me, she has a sense of style. I swear she has hardly changed since those pictures were taken. She's slender, with brown hair just past her shoulders. Where hers is wavy, mine is straight, but her brown eyes match mine perfectly. I know she's family. Considering I've only heard stories about one distant relative, there's no one else she could be.

"Aunt Michelle?" I manage to croak out. My throat is sore and dry. I'm so thirsty.

I push myself up to a sitting position, and I hate every second of moving. But I don't think anything is broken. My aunt holds onto my arm, giving me extra support.

"You can call me Auntie, or Michelle. You don't need to be so formal." She bends down to fluff my pillows, then hugs me gently, if not a little awkwardly.

Her voice is almost familiar. Then I remember why. A month before Mom and I moved, we got a call. I'd answered the phone, and hers was the voice on the line. She called me by name then, but I was too distracted running out the door to wonder about it until later. I wonder why Mom hadn't told me it had been her. I would have liked to talk to her. Then again, I suppose after that call, Mom had been quieter than normal. I didn't want to press her when she seemed to have so much on her mind, so I just never asked. I forgot it soon enough.

"What happened?" I ask. I don't know what hospital this is or how I got here. There's a fog surrounding my mind, making it hard to think.

Michelle frowns, and the fingers of her hand gripping her purse strap tighten until her knuckles lose color. Then she looks up at the doctor as he walks into the room. She doesn't answer my question. I stare at her, waiting for one anyway. But she keeps her gaze locked on the doctor.

My head hurts too much to think clearly.

The doctor—my eyes flick to his name tag: Dr. Underwood—starts talking to my aunt Michelle. After a few seconds, I tune them out, resting my head back against the pillows. I close my eyes, and when I open them again, I'm unsure if several minutes have passed, or just several seconds.

He fusses, and I barely give him a passing glance as he checks my pulse, eyes, throat. He's average height, with salt-and-pepper hair and blue eyes that I'd normally drool over. But not today. Today I just want to keep my head from splitting open from the pain.

Michelle puts her purse in her lap as she sits down on the chair next to my bed, waiting for the doctor to do his thing.

"How do you feel, Miss Price?" he asks.

I hate that my last name is different from Mom's. Always have. I never understood why she gave me my dad's name and not hers, when he hasn't been around since before I was born. Even hyphenating would have been preferable; then at least I could request people use Baker.

I purse my lips and want to give a smart-ass answer, but I hold my tongue. He's only doing his job. Besides, it's only the drumbeat of my pulse pounding at my temples that's making me irritable.

"Not great. My head hurts," I mutter, and because I still want an answer, I add, "What happened?"

"You and your mother were in a car accident, sweetie," Michelle says. The quietness of her voice doesn't suit her.

I jerk up to sit straighter and wince at the pain. "What? Where's Mom? Is she okay?"

My heart thumps, and I can feel each beat hammering in my skull.

Michelle looks to the doctor like she's afraid she's said too much. That look has me worried. *What isn't she telling me? Whatever it is, it can't be good.*

"Can you remember anything about what happened?" the doctor interjects. He must have perfected his bedside manner, because he doesn't look the slightest bit concerned.

I think back. I remember Mom wanting to move to some small town in Colorado I'd never heard of for her job. We were going to stay with an aunt I'd never met before, who is obviously Michelle. I remember packing my things into the car and hoping the movers wouldn't get lost, the vast hours of straight road with next to nothing to look at once we left Oregon, how it was even worse after we crossed through that small corner of Utah, and it was pitch black out with only the blinding headlights from other cars . . . But that's it.

I shake my head, then instantly regret the movement. I hope a nurse comes by with pain meds soon. I don't think I can rest until this pain dies down.

"Don't worry too much about it. You just woke up. Sometimes temporary amnesia of the event can happen. You're very lucky—no broken bones, just some bruising." Dr. Underwood writes on my chart as he talks.

And aching muscles that feel like I've been deadlifting a moose, I think.

"What day is it?" I ask.

"It's the ninth," the doctor says, his pen not even pausing.

It's been two days since we left.

"When can I go home?" I ask. If I have to lay around and be in pain, I'd much rather it be somewhere less sterile looking.

"I would like you to stay the night, but barring any issues, you should be able to go home in the morning."

"What about my mom?" I push. Panic presses down on my chest.

His face is neutral. Not happy, but not the face of having to deliver *really* bad news. "Ms. Baker is stable, but she isn't awake yet, which is for the best. She has quite a few injuries, so we are isolating her for the time being. It will allow her to heal faster without risk of infection. I am confident she'll wake up in the next few days." A strange look passes over his face.

I sit back and breathe. The tightness in my chest eases. Just a bit. She's not in critical condition, so I'm glad for that, though this is far from what I'd hoped to hear.

The doctor puts my chart back at the foot of my bed and says, "I'll be back to check on you later. Visiting hours are only for another few minutes."

Then he leaves the room.

I just want to go home, to sleep in my bed in good old Boring, Oregon. I don't know where we are, but I know this isn't home. "What town are we in?"

Michelle—because even though she's my aunt, I don't know her well enough to think of her like that. Not yet—stands and looks at the clock as she slides the purse strap over a shoulder.

"You're in Havenwood Falls." I must make a face, because she clarifies, "Colorado. The car crashed just outside of Grand Junction, a few hours from here. I had you both brought here when I heard what happened."

I stare dumbly at her. I guess I don't remember *anything* after somewhere in the middle of Wyoming. Did I fall asleep? Mom must have been driving for hours while I was unconscious.

"Get some rest," she says, hugging me again. "I'll be back for you in the morning."

Then she leaves, and I'm alone. I scoot down into the bed, pull a pillow from behind my head, and hug it tightly to my chest.

I don't want to be here, away from my home, my things, and without my mom.

CHAPTER 2

$\mathcal{I}$ wake up feeling heavy, like I slept a long time but somehow still not long enough. I push myself up to sit, thankful my body isn't nearly as sore as yesterday. I wish there was a TV in the room, or at least a halfway decent book. I'd even settle for a school-assigned novel. Not that those have ever been bad—I secretly enjoyed them in the past—they just weren't my preferred taste.

I've already taken one nap since a nurse woke me up this morning to check my vitals.

A nurse or volunteer comes in—I'm not really sure which, because I'm staring at a phone on the wall outside of my room. She drops a tray of food off, then leaves without a word. By the time my brain puts things together enough to say thank you, she's already gone.

I glance at the clock. It's noon, and Michelle isn't here yet. I want to call her, but . . . even if I could get to that phone across the hall, I don't know her number.

I adjust myself to look at the tray. The food doesn't look nearly as bad as people complain about in hospitals, but I don't feel all that hungry. I pick up the spoon and cup of gelatin and frown down at it. Lime. The color reminds me of fresh grass clippings, and though it smells more appetizing, the color is pretty weird. I poke my spoon into it and stir it around. Maybe if I don't look while I eat, it won't be that bad?

I take a bite.

Not great, but I've had worse.

"Sorry I'm late!" Michelle enters in a flurry of movement. She's wearing a pretty pink dress, with knee high boots that don't look like they should work but do, and her hair is pulled back into a cute updo.

I quickly set the toxic-looking food down and push the tray away.

"I got caught up at work and then had to fill out your discharge paperwork." She plops a bag down on a chair. My bag. "I had no idea it would take so long."

"It's okay," I say. She looks at me expectantly. So I blurt the first thing that comes to mind. "Did you know hospitals serve green gelatin because the red flavors are too close to the color of blood, and they need to tell the difference if they need to do emergency surgery?"

She blinks.

Great. She's known me for all of five minutes, and she already thinks I'm weird. Spouting weird facts has always been a mostly bad habit of mine. Mom says I started when I was about five, though even she doesn't know where I picked it up from. I usually do it when I first meet new people or I'm stressed, or really, anytime I'm slightly uncomfortable. Either that or I completely shut down and have a hard time speaking. It always made making friends difficult. That was the one good thing about moving every year or two—I was never in one place long enough to make too much of an impression on anyone.

"I brought your bag for you," Michelle says.

"When can I see Mom?"

A look crosses her face that I don't have time to decipher before it's gone. "I'll go talk to the doctor about that while you get dressed."

If I didn't know better, from the strain in her voice, I'd say there was something that she didn't want me to know. But before I can ask, she's out the door, heading down the hall.

I drop my feet off the edge of the bed and stand. My legs are a little weak, though it's the same feeling I get when I've forgotten to eat all day, so it's manageable.

Opening my bag slumped on the foot of the bed, I rummage around, passing up my jeans for a pair of dark leggings and my Darth Vader sweater. The back of my hand catches the corner of a box I didn't pack. I dig down and pluck it out. It's small, teal, and made of the standard cardboard used for some types of jewelry.

I remove the lid, attaching it to the underside. Inside is a simple, silver bracelet. A tiny star charm, with a chunk of raw amethyst embedded into the center, dangles from one of the links. Mom must have snuck it in my bag as an early birthday present. I clasp it onto my wrist, admiring the glint of light off the polished metal, then shuffle my way to the bathroom to change.

When I look into the mirror, my appearance makes me cringe. My dark brown hair is in tangles, so I work my fingers through, combing it back as best I can.

Michelle is back when I emerge from the bathroom. She's smiling and holding my bag. "The doctor says we can visit Angela in a few days. He just wants her to heal a little more first."

It's not bad news, I tell myself. I'll be able to see her soon enough. We've been apart for longer periods of time than that when she goes on her business trips.

Michelle leads me out to her car. As we exit the building, a blast of cold air hits me. It's the middle of the day, with a little wind and full sun, yet I swear my breath froze before it even had a chance to exit my body. I crinkle my nose, rubbing it with the back of my hand to rid myself of the odd sensation. I was not built for this kind of weather.

The drive is mostly silent. Sleep weighs on me even though I've been sleeping for days.

I look at Michelle from the corners of my eyes. But she continues talking, not leaving me with an opening, telling me about the bakery she owns, Daily Knead. I'm too tired to really focus on her words or respond with more than grunts and nods anyway. Instead, I watch the town pass. Everything is so close together.

Michelle turns onto a street leading up to a small neighborhood.

"Welcome to Havenstone," she says as we pass a sign stating as much.

The houses are cute and remind me of a ski resort you'd see in TV shows. The roofs are steep, and the wood has been sanded and polished to accentuate the lines and knots of the trees they were made from. Michelle puts the car in park in front of one with dark-stained wood.

Inside, her place is warm and cozy. An overstuffed couch sits under a window, the fireplace is on the far right wall, and two very comfortable-looking chairs, with thick fur-like blankets draped over the backs, sit near the back wall of the room. The floors are hardwood, a light honey color with rugs strategically placed. That will be nice in the mornings.

It surprises me a little that she doesn't live in a bigger place. Not that she needs one, but with her corporate hairstyle and heels, I'd expected her home to look like it came out of a magazine. You'd think she lived in a bubble of spring while the rest of the world is in the middle of what has to be an unusually arctic winter.

Looking out the window, I frown at the snow. I much prefer rainy winters.

I wander into the dining room on the left. It's small and simple, with a round wooden table pushed against the wall. There's a swinging door that I assume leads into the kitchen.

"Your great-grandfather made that," Michelle says to me from behind. She nods toward the table. I smile and move back into the main living area. She walks around me, motioning down the hall, and shows me to my room. "I've made up the guest room for you until your mother gets out of the hospital. Then we can go house-hunting together."

I just nod.

We pass a closed door, which I assume is Michelle's room, and an office with a large desk and shelves of books lining one wall.

Once we get to my temporary room, I drop my bag at the foot of the bed and plop down onto my back, ready to take a nap. *How can I still be so tired?*

"Don't fall asleep just yet. I'm expecting company soon, then I'll make lunch." And with that, she is off down the hall. Again, I can't shake the feeling that there's something she's not telling me.

My eyelids droop. This mattress is too comfortable. I could curl up and hibernate straight through the rest of winter. Somehow, though, I manage to find it in me to roll off the bed and stand before I fall asleep. I stretch, then make my way out into the hall. My feet stop in mid-stride when I see a painting.

There's nothing remarkable about it, though it has a Bob Ross feel to it. The image is of a forest, but one seemingly out-of-place detail sticks out. I squint at the figure. A man standing in the distance. He looks like he doesn't belong, like someone added him years later, only with paints that weren't nearly as vibrant. The style in which he's painted is more detailed, and less free-flowing than the rest.

"Mason, your father, painted that years ago, before you were born," Michelle says.

You mean, before he left us, I think bitterly. My reply dies on my tongue as I jump, startled by the knock on the door.

An hour later, I'm sitting on the couch, staring at my aunt like she's grown two extra heads. Which, given what just happened, would be slightly less weird. When she said *company*, I didn't expect to get a tattoo. I'm a minor, for crap's sake. I side-eye Michelle. Last I checked, that wasn't exactly legal. Something about wards and protections. I don't know. It doesn't make much sense to me still.

"So your mother didn't tell you?" she asks, gripping the back of a chair. Though her expression is calm and slightly confused, her knuckles are white from the strain.

I shake my head slowly. Either I'm insane . . . or she is. Either way, I'm stuck here in a tiny town in the middle of the Rocky Mountains with no one to save me.

"Nope," I say, hoping I'm doing a decent job at hiding my worry. My eyes are wide, so probably not.

Michelle paces the room for a minute, then sits down next to me and takes my hands in hers. "We are witches. The tattoo is to help keep your powers under control as they come in. I know it's hard to believe, but . . ." She trails off and studies my face for a moment. "I think it will be easier to show you."

She waves her hand at the fireplace and snaps her fingers. Instantly, a roaring fire starts up.

I jump up on the couch, pulling my knees to my chest. The skin on my right shoulder, where I got my tattoo, stings a little from the movement. "What. The. Crap!"

Try as I might, there's no explanation I can come up with to explain how she did that—not any that doesn't involve magic. I blow out a breath. Magic . . . witches . . .

"Does Mom know?" I ask.

She laughs and moves to sit next to me. "Of course. Your mother is a witch, too. We tend not to use our powers like that, and never in public."

"So what? Is this town some kind of witchy sanctuary?" I ask.

Michelle reaches for my hand, but I jerk it back. She takes the hint and scoots away, giving me a little more room. "Not exactly. There are a lot of different supes in this town. Shifters, witches like us, some witches with vastly different types of magic, fae, and more."

I think she stopped at *more* to spare me further insanity.

"Shifters? Like . . . werewolves?"

"Wolves, dragons, and—"

"Dragons?" I snort. "You know this sounds absolutely insane, right?"

"I know. It will take some getting used to. But there are also humans in town, though most aren't aware of us."

"Is it even safe to go outside?" I can feel my eyes about to pop out of my head.

She laughs. "Of course it is. We live here because it's safe." Michelle lowers her voice. "I'm sorry. I never realized Angela didn't tell you. That's why the two of you moved here, because your powers will be coming in on your birthday, which also happens to be on the night of the supermoon. And because our power is drawn from the moon, your powers will be the strongest our family has seen in generations."

"I think I'm going to be sick." This has to be a joke. I mean, there's no such thing as witches like she's trying to get me to believe.

Yet, I saw her light that fire. No hidden button, no remote. Just a snap of her finger. This is crazy, and what's worse is that I find myself starting to believe her.

"I will help you as your powers manifest," she goes on.

All I can do is nod, hugging my knees to my chest as she keeps talking. But I've stopped listening. Her voice is just a muffled buzz in my head. I'm feeling completely overwhelmed, and I can feel myself shutting down. The emotions are too thick and they steal my words, my voice . . . and I don't know how I'll ever find either again.

This cannot be real.

CHAPTER 3

"Are you okay?" Michelle asks. I startle at her touch, and she quickly withdraws her hand from my shoulder.

I dig deep, and try for something simple.

"I think so?" I manage to say, though it's more question than confirmation. My head is caught in a fog. It has to be shock.

She looks at me. "Are you sure? You've been sitting there staring at the wall for a good twenty minutes."

She sets down a tray on the coffee table in front of me, with two cups and a teapot with steam swirling up from the spout.

I drop my knees, bringing my feet to the floor. "So the town is full of witches . . ."

"And shifters, fae, angels, and—" She cuts herself off when she sees my incredulous expression.

My emotions have calmed some, so I think of something to say . . . anything. But what comes out is, "Did you know that no one knows where the word *witch* originated from?" I nod as if she answered. "Yeah, there are several words that could have led to it. There are three Old English words it could have come from, meaning 'female sorceress,' or the word meaning 'divination' or the one meaning 'idol.' There's also the Germanic word that means 'one who wakes the dead.'"

Apparently my report on the Salem witch trials back in the eighth grade stuck with me more than I thought.

Sorceress . . . divination . . . idol . . . waking the dead . . . These words are too heavy for me, and suddenly I'm overwhelmed again. I press my lips in a tight line.

Michelle is silent for a minute before she shakes her head and laughs as if I told a joke. "I didn't know that. Why don't you unpack, and I'll make you something to eat—"

"I think I need some air." I stand up a little too fast. My head spins, and I have to grab the arm of the couch.

"You probably shouldn't. You just got home from the hospital." She jerks her chin toward the kitchen. "And lunch will be ready in a few minutes. I'm making enchiladas."

The warm smell of seasonings and chicken wafts through the room, making my mouth water. Food is the last thing on my mind right now. And though I am hungry, what she told me has formed a pit of nerves in my stomach, and I'm not sure I could eat a single bite.

"I'm fine," I say as calmly as I can. Though really, this is too much to take in all at once, and I just need time, *alone*, to let it sink in.

Maybe she sees something in my eyes, because she says, "All right, I can drop you off in town for an hour or so."

"Nope, no. It's only a few blocks. I can walk." I'm being rude. I know I am. Mom raised me better than this. Guilt creeps in, but I push it away.

"Normally, I would let you, but considering your head injury, I'd feel better taking you. Besides, Angela would kill me if I let you walk. Here's a cell. I programmed my number in there. Just call when you're ready to be picked up. You'll also need a jacket."

I think about refusing, only for a moment. She's family, and insane or not, she's only tried to help me and take care of me so far. "Thanks," I mutter.

Michelle stands. "Clarke, I know this is probably a lot to take in, but we can talk more about it later."

More? How much more could there be?

She hurries to the office and is back in seconds with a warm wool jacket with large pearl buttons and knee-high boots that somehow are both practical and stylish. Maybe I should have her help me pick out a winter wardrobe, because I'm going to need it. None of my winter clothes are made for winters below an average of forty-five degrees.

∼

After Michelle drives off, I turn in a slow circle, looking at my surroundings. There are a few people out running errands or walking leisurely with friends. I scan the businesses, and my eyes catch on the coffee shop across the street. Coffee Haven.

Good, I could use something to warm me up. I'm practically an ice cube from standing outside for less than five minutes. I cross the street and head in.

Instantly I'm surrounded by warmth and the heavenly aroma of freshly ground coffee. I take a deep breath and savor the bright scent. The setup is similar to most coffee shops, but it has a much friendlier vibe than those chain stores. Art lines the walls, some of them watercolors. The use of brush strokes and how the artist mastered using each color in a variety of ways make me wish I had a fraction of their talent. My eyes linger on the portrait of a platinum-blond-haired woman near the bar. I wonder who she is to be given such a prominent place.

Hanging plants and crystals spread around the place give it a personal touch and make it feel homey. It reminds me of Oregon. I think I found my new favorite place.

There isn't much of a line, so I stride over to the long marble counter that reminds me of an old-timey ice cream shop. I take my time scanning the menu. In the end, I settle on the same thing I get every time I'm at any coffee place.

"Next."

I blink and realize it's my turn. A girl about my age, with shoulder-length dark-sand-colored hair and honey eyes looks at me expectantly. She's so skinny, and I have the urge to knit her a massive scarf. She doesn't say anything else, but I know she's waiting on me. Her name tag reads *Roxanne*. There's a book on the counter next to her, and I try to peek at the title, but can't see it from where I stand.

"One large hot chocolate with extra whipped cream—" My stomach growls loudly. I give Roxanne a sheepish look and add, "and a blueberry scone, please."

She rings me up, and I dig through my bag until I find my wallet, then hand over my cash. My fingers drum on the marble.

"Here you go," she says and hands me my change. "You can get your order when it's ready over there." Roxanne points down the counter. As my gaze follows where she points, I can't help but notice some scarring peeking out from the cuff of her sleeve. I wonder what happened. I feel rude for staring, so I push it from my mind. It's not my business.

"Thanks," I say, taking a step back.

The heel of my boot slides on melted snow I'd managed to drag in. As I stumble, my back collides with something hard. Two large hands come down on my shoulders to steady me. I freeze, not moving. The hands push me forward a step, and I nearly stumble again. *Would* have stumbled if he'd let go right away. Tilting my chin up, I look over my shoulder and up the massive chest to a painfully handsome face. Heat rises up my neck.

"Sorry," I say slowly, with a hint of a question mark thrown in. Slow enough to make me come across as slightly unhinged. My brain has gone slack from just looking into his eyes. *My* eyes are brown— these are something in another league altogether. An amber, *almost* brown, only with too much gold to be called something so . . . normal. They remind me of the setting sun.

I know I'm staring, but I've never been so attracted to a total stranger before in my life. It's textbook romance novel, and even in my half-drooling state, I know it's the ultimate cheesefest. I probably have little cartoon hearts over my eyes.

When he finally removes his hands from my person, I notice he's frowning at me, almost sneering. "You should watch where you're going" is all he says. He lets out an annoyed huff I don't think I was meant to hear, then moves around me, all but pushing me out of his way like I was a stray dog.

The cartoon eye hearts pop, and my attraction to him curdles like milk. *What a jerk!*

The barista places my order on the counter, and I snatch it up and storm over to a free table in the corner near a window.

Great first impression. I hope not everyone is as rude as he is. I already hate being here. Picked up in the middle of the school year and dragged to a place with winters that would make a polar bear hate life, with an aunt who was clearly losing her mind . . .

No, that's not fair. I know what she showed me was real, but it's still hard to wrap my mind around. And there was that tattoo lady . . . So maybe I'm stuck in a nightmare, losing *my* mind, and have created this white hell for myself. A cute little suburb that looks peaceful and sweet, but nothing good is waiting for me.

As much as I want to be mad at Mom for moving us to a tiny town in the middle of nowhere, I can't. Not when she's still in the hospital.

I twist a strand of hair around my finger and tug. I hope she wakes up soon.

That guy's voice breaks through my thoughts. I chomp down angrily on my scone, staring out the window and still seething. I force myself to keep my gaze on the world outside, refusing to give him a second's attention. Who says *watch it* when a stranger clearly accidentally bumps into them? It's not like I meant to do it, and I even apologized.

A chair at the table next to me scoots out with a screech, drawing my attention away from the snowy town. I nearly choke on my bite when I see his face.

Did he seriously sit down in front of me just to openly glare? Another guy, his friend, I'm guessing, takes a seat in the chair next to him, but I don't notice much more than that with those amber eyes bearing down on me. Why won't he look away already?

I take an angry sip of my hot chocolate and sputter when I burn my tongue. He's smirking now. It's childish, but I'm in such a foul

ALI WINTERS

mood that I don't care. I stick out my tongue and make a face, which only makes his smirk grow bigger.

I sniff, catching the scent of pennies, but it's gone before I can be sure. It's probably my insanity catching up with me.

I look away and eye the shops across from here, pausing when my gaze passes an old man standing directly across the street, staring right at me. I shake my head. No, from the look of him, he's probably just cold and hungry and staring at the café itself. His clothes are the kind of dark that happens to previously bright colors when they are covered in dirt and stains, and aged from wear.

Reaching into my pocket, I look at my change. I don't have enough left to buy him anything, but he might appreciate what I do have to give.

With Mr. Glares-a-lot so close, there's no way I can sit and enjoy my scone and hot chocolate anyway. I stuff the pastry in my mouth as I get to my feet, snatching up my drink and throwing my bag over my shoulder, then storm out into the chilly afternoon air.

The man is gone now. I scan the street and don't see him anywhere. I guess I was wrong.

As distracting as the rude guy was, I'm still not ready to go back to Michelle's place. Everything she told me is still swimming around in my head.

Shoving the change back into my pocket, I take the pastry hanging out of my mouth and hold it in my hand, then wander up and down the street for a while, window shopping, as I finish my scone. My hot chocolate cools off way too fast. I pass Summit Jewelers, ogling their window display and the array of beautiful designs.

When I move on, I manage to find a bookstore on the far side of the square. I look behind me, trying to remember the name of the bookstore next to Coffee Haven. I make note of them, planning to visit when I have more money. I'm almost finished with my current book and will need a new one soon. I stand in front of Into the Mystic New Age Books and Gifts, and I wonder if they have anything on witches.

I feel a pull to go in. My hand hovers inches away from the door

18

handle, but just before I move to go in, a wave of . . . something hits me. It's a lot like being dizzy, only not. I don't know how to explain it. Something more overwhelming than that, something with a deep unidentifiable emotion attached to it. I shiver, suddenly feeling like I'm being watched.

Looking around, I don't see anyone, other than a few people running in and out of stores from their cars.

I check the cell Michelle gave me. I've been gone for a few hours. Even I can admit I've calmed down enough to go back. Even if I haven't, the cold is enough to make me call it quits. The cold air might hurt my face, but walking around in it certainly helped clear my head. Though I can't see how this witch thing will sort itself out in my mind for some time, I think I am ready to talk about it more.

So I shoot Michelle a text.

Clarke: I'm ready to be picked up.

A few minutes later it dings in my hand.

Michelle: I'm stuck at work, there was a minor emergency. Just got a last minute order. I can pick you up in an hour or two.

Michelle: Unless you want to walk here?

Clarke: Is it close to where you dropped me off?

I wait a few minutes before it pings again with directions. It doesn't seem as close as I would have liked, but I've walked farther over the past few hours, so it isn't a big deal.

Ten minutes later, I am freezing my toes off as I walk up to the storefront. A wooden sign is mounted above the door made of polished wood with simple deep blue lettering. I push open the glass door with my backside, rubbing my arms with my hands. A bell rings above my head. I don't see my aunt anywhere . . . but I do see *him*.

My hands still. His are splayed across the countertop, and Mr. Glares-a-lot is looking down his nose, giving me an expression I interpret as him feeling superior.

A blush crawls up my neck and burns my cheeks.

"Are you following me now?" he asks.

CHAPTER 4

"What? No, of course not!" I hiss, approaching the counter and barely keeping my voice from raising. The last thing I want to do is draw the attention of everyone in the dining area to the scene I'm sure we're making. "This is my aunt's store."

As soon as those words leave my mouth, he cringes before he can school his features. I note it with a little more satisfaction than I should.

There's a smear of flour on his cheek. He must have been working in the back. He looks at me for a few seconds longer, head cocked to the side, then goes back to work wiping down the counter and cleaning up, effectively ignoring me.

I fiddle with the bracelet around my wrist. It's strangely warm against my skin. Then again, I'm so cold right now, I'm not surprised the metal is doing a better job of holding heat than I am.

"Will you please let my aunt know I'll be waiting outside?" I ask through my teeth, trying to keep my voice as pleasant as possible.

He looks at me in a way I can't decipher, then goes into the back room without a word. Closing my eyes, I count to five and take in a slow, measured breath. I tried to be nice. I really did. It's a mystery why Michelle would want to hire someone with such a sour disposition.

The frigid air hits my face with an icy blast as I go back outside. I end up pacing the parking lot of the shopping plaza in an attempt to keep warm. It doesn't work as well as I would have liked. The light from the sun is fading fast, thanks to the towering mountains swallowing up a good bit of sky.

That guy's face flashes in my mind. I don't know why I let him get under my skin like this. I don't know how he can when we've never even held a conversation. He's a total stranger I had no idea existed before a few hours ago. I'm going to be eighteen in a few days. Yet somehow he manages to make me feel like a cranky child who missed her nap.

A shiver works its way down my body. I continue pacing and rub my hands up and down my arms. When I look up from the ground, I see the old man again, across the street in front of the high school. I glance around. This is definitely a different street. What an odd coincidence.

It's strange that he'd be out here when the temperature is quickly dropping. Then again, so am I. The difference is that I have somewhere to go, where I can only assume he doesn't.

Remembering the change in my pocket, I decide now is as good a time as any to give it to him. I rub my nose, trying to get the sudden sharp tang of copper out of my nostrils. I'm pretty sure the cold is somehow messing with my sense of smell.

The street is quiet, so I take a step toward him, my foot just touching the asphalt of the street when I am jerked back into a hard body. A car drives by a second later, kicking up a small wave of snow slush.

"Are you *trying* to get yourself killed?" Mr. Cranky grunts. I really should learn his name, but it doesn't really matter, I suppose. I don't exactly plan on becoming BFFs with him.

When I don't say anything, he lets me go, crossing his arms over his chest. He shifts his weight and cocks his head. Waiting.

It takes a few seconds before I can get my brain and mouth to sync up enough to answer him. I blink. The man is gone, and the car that nearly hit me is driving down the road, snow sloshing beneath the tires.

"I-I didn't see it! There weren't any cars around a second ago."

His liquid amber eyes narrow. I'm not sure he believes me. "Michelle asked me to come get you. She said she was going to be too long and doesn't want you to freeze."

His tone is softer than I expected, so I let him guide me back inside. I can't help but notice his hand stays on my lower back the entire time. He's so warm, it's hard to avoid leaning into him. Part of me is relieved he came to get me. I don't think I would have lasted much longer outside.

His hand doesn't leave me until he pulls out a chair at a small table in the back and motions for me to sit. Then he's gone, and I'm left to entertain myself until Michelle is ready.

I trace the lines of wood on the table with my finger for a few minutes before pulling my book out of my bag and opening it. I flip through the pages, removing the bookmark, and get lost within the words. The murmur of other patrons' conversations surrounds me in a sea of white noise.

A white ceramic mug with a mountain of whipped cream on top jolts me out of the story. I slam the book closed and look up, startled to see *him* of all people.

"Here" is all he says. But he doesn't leave. We just look at each other for a long moment. Then he rolls his eyes and lets out an exaggerated sigh, setting a cookie down next to the mug on top of a folded white napkin.

Perhaps this is a peace offering? Either that or my aunt is making him be nice. I look from the cookie to his face, meaning to say thanks, though what comes out instead is, "The average American will eat thirty-five *thousand* cookies in their lifetime."

I can't believe I just said that. I reach up and tug on a strand of hair. If I'm not mistaken, the corner of his mouth twitches in what I can only assume is an attempt to hide a smirk. When he doesn't move or speak, I say, "I'm Clarke."

"I know," he says, then, "Seth."

There's no offering of a handshake from either us. I suppose we'll take this one baby step at a time then. The smear of flour from earlier is still there on his face.

"Do you want to sit down?" I ask hesitantly. Though I'm not sure I actually want him to.

Using the toe of my boot, I scoot the chair across from me out as much as I can. His gaze bounces from the chair to my face a few times. He opens his mouth, and I think he's about to accept, but there's a clatter in the back room that draws our attention away from each other.

He shakes his head and jerks a thumb over his shoulder. "Looks like I might be needed in the back, then I need to start the prep for the morning shift."

It's the most words he's said to me since we met. And the nicest. I look at him, not sure what to say to that. And when I take too long, he walks away.

Great. He's trying, and I ruin it by not speaking.

I finish my drink and cookie while pretending to read. I can't focus anymore and keep stealing glances at him from the corner of my vision as he mans the register and cleans between customers.

By the time he leaves, jacket in hand, the store is otherwise deserted. I think about running over to apologize. He's too fast, and before I can make up my mind to actually do it, the door is closing behind him. I'll thank him for the peace offering the next time I see him.

A few minutes later, Michelle finally comes out of the back room.

"Sorry that took so long," Michelle says as she approaches. She pauses in the middle of the dining area and looks around as if she expected something completely different.

The drive home is mostly silent. The cold has zapped any energy I'd had, and I'm ready for bed. I trudge up the steps into the house behind Michelle. She has a lot of energy still, and I'm super jealous.

"I can have dinner ready in about an hour," she says as she unlocks the front door.

"Thanks," I say, "but I think I just want to head to bed."

She nods understandingly. "There will be a plate in the fridge if you wake up and decide you're hungry."

Then she flits off toward the kitchen while I make my way down the hall. I pass the painting and look at the faded man with an arm raised, as if he were caught jumping up and down.

"Even you seem to have more energy than I do right now," I mutter to him.

My exhaustion must be getting to me because I could have sworn he was a little smaller and just standing when I'd looked earlier.

I shake it off and then make my way to my room, dropping facedown onto my mattress. Though I'm exhausted, the events of the day swirl though my mind. How could I have missed that car? I'm lucky Seth was around, otherwise I'd be frozen roadkill right now . . . then there was the peace offering. What could that have meant? Am I reading too much into a cookie?

But underneath it all, I find myself believing what Michelle told me is true, despite not having witnessed any sign of magic since she demonstrated hers for me.

I am a witch.

CHAPTER 5

*L*ight filters in through the window. I crane my neck to look at the clock on the nightstand next to my bed. It's almost half past eight, which means I've been sleeping for over twelve hours. I force myself to sit up. The thick pink blanket, which Michelle must have draped over me, slides to the floor.

I'm still a little achy, though not nearly what I felt like yesterday or the day before.

Walking like a zombie, I fumble my way to the dining room to find Michelle fully dressed and drinking tea as she reads the paper. I've never met anyone more put together than this woman.

"Good morning, Clarke, would you like some tea or coffee?"

I shake my head and spot a box of cereal on the counter. "No, thanks, I'm just going to have some of this," I say, grabbing it and setting it on the table before I go into the kitchen to grab the milk.

When I get back, a bowl and spoon already wait for me on the table. Michelle is tidying up the counters, and when I finish pouring my cereal, she takes the box and milk away. After skipping dinner last night, I am famished. I start shoveling spoonfuls of cereal into my mouth while she washes her mug.

"I was thinking about going for a walk later," I say between mouthfuls. "I'm still a little sore, but I think moving will help."

"That's a good idea. Be sure to take your phone in case you need anything. I'll be at the bakery for most of the day again."

Lifting the bowl to my mouth, I drink the leftover milk, then walk to the sink and wash my dishes while my aunt dries them.

"I can drop you off in town," Michelle offers, leaning a hip against the counter.

"That would be great, thanks."

She wipes her hands on a dish towel and folds it. Setting it down, she turns to face me. "I almost forgot. I had your car towed and am having the windows replaced. The mechanic said there wasn't much damage, so we'll be able to pick it up soon."

I swallow, not entirely sure I feel like getting into that particular car again anytime soon. "You don't have to do that," I protest.

"Nonsense, you will need a car to get around while I'm at work, and when Angela gets home, she'll need it as well."

I smile at her practicality. "Well, thank you."

Michelle crosses to me and kisses the top of my head. "Okay, go get ready, then."

I hurry down the hall back to my temporary room to get dressed. I pull out an outfit from my bag. I'll need to unpack when I get back. There's no telling when Mom and I will have our own place. That, and living out of a suitcase sucks.

Picking an oversized gray sweater and some colorful leggings that match the boots Michelle let me borrow yesterday, I make my way to the shower, throwing my hair up into a messy bun.

I turn the water up as high as I can stand, soaking up as much of the warmth as possible. I could stay standing under the water all day as the practically scalding temperature soothes my muscles, but Michelle is waiting for me, so I force myself to hurry.

By the time I get back to the front room, I realize I've taken longer than intended. Though there's not an ounce of impatience in her, I apologize. She brushes it off, saying she doesn't mind, and we head out.

The car is already running as we walk outside. I appreciate the warmth blasting from the vents.

"Most people will be at work or school, so if you get bored, you can come by the bakery and hang out," Michelle says as I buckle myself in.

"Would it be okay if I went there with you before I go into town?"

Michelle smiles knowingly. "Seth isn't working today."

Heat prickles at my chest and works its way up my neck to my face. I push my mortification from my mind. That isn't what I'd meant at all. I clear my throat.

"Do you think we can visit Mom soon?" I ask quietly.

She taps her palm against her forehead. "Oh, I meant to tell you earlier, Dr. Underwood said we could visit her Wednesday of next week."

"Really?" I ask a little louder than I meant to. While I'm glad I will get to see her, it's not as soon as I had hoped. Wednesday was the day after my birthday. It will be the first birthday without her. I shake away my sad thoughts and tell myself that we can celebrate it another time together.

Then I turn and watch the neighborhood go by, covered in snow and decorated with pink and red hearts and cupids. With the move and the car wreck, I've completely forgotten about Valentine's Day.

Beautiful aspen trees are nestled into the landscape, and fit so perfectly with everything it almost looks as if someone placed each and every one of them in a specific spot. Not even a fake town could look half as perfectly put together.

The drive is shorter than it felt last night. I probably could have walked, but I think I'd like to get to know Michelle a little better. Even though I have about a million questions, I appreciate that she's not pushing the witch thing on me. I want to talk about it, but the idea is just so . . . unbelievable. I feel like Darrin did in that classic TV show Mom and I used to watch together when I was growing up, *Bewitched.* Except I guess, in this case, I'm Samantha.

We walk into Daily Knead, and there is a short line and several people sitting at various tables, eating.

Michelle walks straight toward the back, greeting everyone as she walks past them. It's the kind of thing I've only seen in Hallmark movies. Everyone seems to know everyone. I look around at the faces and wonder how long it will be until I know every face by heart.

A woman with a blond bob is at the register, helping the short line of people. I get in line, and it's not long before it's my turn. I order a large tea, then head to a small two-person table along the back wall. I dig out my book from my bag and open it to where I left off, getting lost in the words.

Flipping the last page and reading the conclusion I had been hoping for, I let loose a contented sigh. I close my book and stand, stretching my back, then glance at the clock. Nearly noon. I've been reading for most of the morning.

The sun shines brightly outside and reflects off the snow, making the day brighter than normal. With the breakfast crowd gone and the lunch crowd not yet starting, the place is nearly empty. Walking toward the counter, I lean over. Michelle spots me and waves. I motion toward the door indicating that I'm heading out for my walk, and wave my phone. She smiles and nods.

I take off and look at Havenwood Falls High School in the distance. I think I'm actually looking forward to starting school. While I enjoy my alone time, I miss being around other people as well. It would be nice to know others my age, and maybe if I'm lucky, I'll have time to make some friends before summer break.

I cross the parking lot and head farther into the city, ending up at the town square across from City Hall. Covered in snow, it looks like a postcard. The cold sucks big time, but this town still manages to be beautiful, even with the pink and red Valentine's Day decorations that are everywhere.

Pulling my cell from my bag, I snap a few pictures. I'll show Mom once she wakes up. I pause and suck in a shuddering breath, suddenly filled with overwhelming uncertainty. It takes several inhales before I calm my anxiety and remind myself that Michelle will be calling the doctor today, and we'll get an update.

I continue walking the parameter of the square, snapping pictures of the town and the mountains surrounding it. In the distance, I hear the sound of a bell ringing. The high school must be out for the day.

Just shy of completing my first round, a wave of dizziness washes over me, and for half a second, I'm not sure which way is up or which is down. The tang of copper twinges in my nose. I stumble as my foot catches on a small chunk of hardened snow. I grunt, barely regaining my balance in time to avoid falling.

Snow crunches underfoot, like I'm stepping on piles of tiny bones. It's a morbid thought, not the type I tend to gravitate toward. I screw up my nose and brush off the thought as a side effect of the dizzy spell. A shudder skitters along my skin as I try to shake the thought away while I make my way to the nearest bench. I dust the thin layer of snow off and take a seat, super glad it's not made of metal.

That was so weird. I rub my temples with my fingers. I'm probably pushing myself too hard without realizing it. Or the cold is getting to me more than I thought.

Deciding to stay on the bench for a few minutes before I try to get up again, I scroll through the pictures I took. After going through the first few, I squint, taking a closer look at them. There's a man in the background of several of them, always looking toward the camera.

I snap my head up and scan the park in that area. He's there, across from me, near the gazebo, leaning on a tree and smoking a cigarette. I'm overcome with self-consciousness because I swear it seems like he's watching me. In reality, I'm sure he's waiting for a wife or girlfriend to show up . . . but it seems strange to meet someone so early in a park. Of course, it's a possibility he's just on a break.

Or maybe, I think, letting my imagination run away, *he's a spy waiting for his secret informant, who may or may not be hiding in the tree like the spy from my favorite sixties TV show,* Get Smart.

I laugh to myself and stand, feeling more stable than I was a few minutes ago. I think I'll call it a day on this walk and just head back to Daily Knead.

I don't manage to take more than five steps before I slip on black ice. I'm falling and hitting the hard ground before I know what's happening. And my ankle is screaming.

"Frick, frick, frick!" I say through clenched teeth, as I clutch at the throbbing pain.

Somehow, I manage to hobble around the patch of ice and back to the bench, swearing up a storm the entire way.

"I don't know why Michelle lets you go off without a babysitter," a warm voice says close behind me. There's a hint of annoyance in the teasing words. Warmth brushes across my skin, making several hairs that escaped my bun move, tickling my neck.

"Excuse me?" I seethe, turning to face Seth. He's much closer than I thought, and I swallow.

"Look at you." He waves a hand toward my leg, smiling an ever so slightly crooked grin. Seth folds his arms along the back of the bench, hovering over my shoulder. His face is only a few short inches from mine. Close enough that when he talks, I can feel his warm breath brush my cheek. I snap my face forward, looking straight at the ground. "A few hours on your own, and you slip and fall on the smallest patch of ice in this town."

He's teasing me, but I feel so overwhelmed with everything. A new place, a new school, no friends within a thousand miles, my mom still in the hospital, and I can't even visit her yet . . . and I keep bumping into this jerk. His attempts at humor are falling wide of their goal.

"Just go away," I mutter. I don't want to look at him. I don't want him to know that if I blink, I might just start crying. This vulnerable feeling snuck up on me. Though I suppose it's been there this entire time. The pain in my ankle and his pathetic attempts at humor seem to be the final straws.

The more I think about it, the more I find myself unable to speak. And the fact that he's here right now, bugging me and forcing me to tell him to leave me alone, infuriates me.

Everything is too much. The emotions in me are too strong, making me want to close my mouth and never speak again.

I hate that I shut down. But even more, I hate that he's forcing me to fight it. It keeps the emotions too raw. My hands ball into fists on my knees.

Then I feel him sidle up to me on the bench.

"Get up," he says.

"Go. Away." I fold my arms over my chest, twisting away from him.

"Come on, I'll help you walk back."

Why won't he just take a hint? It's like he's trying to push all my buttons.

"No, thank you," I insist.

He waits a few beats, then takes my arm and lifts me by the elbow with a gentle but firm grip. "You can't just sit here all day. Your aunt would be pissed if I didn't take you back."

"She can't fire you for that." I snort derisively at him.

"I know," he says. "That's not what I'm worried about."

I narrow my eyes at him for a long moment, debating how stubborn I feel like being today. I try to distract him. "Did you know one of Saturn's moons has an ice volcano?"

"No. That's . . . *weird.*" He clears his throat. "Are you ready to go now?"

He holds out a hand. I stare at it like it might bite me, then grudgingly, I take it and let him loop an arm around my waist while I stretch mine to get it over his shoulder. I don't even try to talk to him on the way back. If I didn't need his help, I would have stayed on that bench until he went away.

Being so close to him feels strange. I kind of hate that I *don't* hate it. He has this relaxing woodsy scent, something like wood smoke and dark chocolate. As we walk, I occasionally test out my ankle. Each time, a stabbing pain shoots up my leg, and Seth practically growls, snapping at me to stop doing that.

We don't reach the bakery fast enough for my liking.

As soon as we enter Daily Knead, I remove my arm from his shoulder and push his arm from around my waist. I hobble to the counter and get in line. Lucky for me, there's only one person ahead of me. I use the counter for support as I advance. Seth is standing inches away. He probably thinks I'm going to fall.

"Welcome to Daily Knead." A girl's chipper voice calls my attention away from Seth. Her name tag reads *Meghan.* She's slender, with her dark hair pulled back into a ponytail. Meghan gives me a broad smile that reaches her dark eyes.

"Can I get a hot chocolate with extra whipped cream?" I ask.

"Sure thing!" Meghan rings me up while I fish for my wallet in my bag. "You're new here, aren't you?"

"Yeah, I'm registering at Havenwood Falls High later this week." Then after a moment I say, "I'm Clarke."

Meghan's smile broadens. "Really? Maybe we'll have a few classes together! I'm Meghan." She points to her name tag, then her smile falters for half a second, and she asks, "Clarke? Michelle's Clarke?"

There's something incredibly infectious about her attitude. I can feel the stress of starting at another school start to melt with just a few words.

"Yeah." It's a strange feeling to be recognized for a change.

"Are you going to the Sweetheart Dance?" Meghan asks, her eyes flicking toward Seth.

Warmth blooms across my face. "Probably not. I don't start school until next week." The words come out in a rush. I can almost feel Seth's eyes on me.

Seth's arm reaches between us and hands Meghan the cash for my drink. I scowl at him, then look past, realizing I'm holding up the line. So I keep my comments to myself. Meghan hands me my drink and says, "Well, hope to see you around!"

"Yeah!" I agree. "I look forward to it."

Seth grabs my drink before I can and stretches out his arm toward the tables. I hobble to one and plop down in the chair. He sets my drink down, then leaves without a word, my "thank you" dying on my lips. I just don't understand that guy at all. He's both helpful and annoyed at the same time.

I sip my hot chocolate, nearly burning my tongue. I can feel his eyes on me from a few tables over. But I do my best to ignore him.

CHAPTER 6

I shift, making the tissue paper crinkle on the exam table. My hands are folded in my lap, and I lace and unlace my fingers. My aunt is in the chair in the corner, reading a magazine. My hands feel clammy, and I don't know why I'm so nervous. The only sound in the room is the ticking of the clock and the sound of pages turning.

The room is as nondescript as it can get. It looks like every other examination room in every other medical facility. White walls, table and furniture with blue faux-leather material, a blue privacy curtain . . . Just once, I wonder what it would be like to see a daffodil yellow curtain, a mural of a forest along one wall . . .

Bored, I swing my legs, and wince. As long as I don't move my ankle, it feels fine now. I hate to admit it, but I'm glad Seth found me when he did and helped me back to the bakery. I didn't realize how cold it was until he held me to his side. I feel heat bloom across my cheeks thinking about it.

Dr. Underwood walks in, grabbing my chart from the back of the door.

"How are you doing today, Ms. Price?" he asks, sitting down on the cushioned rolling stool. He flips through the intake form, scanning the information.

"I'm okay, I guess," I say. "I slipped on some ice and twisted my ankle." It even feels stupid saying it. But it could be worse. I could have fallen on my face and cracked a tooth. Just the idea of breaking a tooth sends a shudder along my body.

Setting the paper down and taking notes, he says, "Why don't you take off your sock and shoe and roll up your pant leg."

I oblige, setting the single shoe next to me.

"All right," he says, scooting over to me and lifting my leg by the back of my calf muscle. His gloved fingers test the skin around my ankle, then the ankle itself. "Does this hurt?"

I shake my head no. He rotates my ankle, and I hiss through my teeth when he fully extends it.

Then he gently sets my ankle down and tells me I can put my sock and shoe back on. He scoots back to the desk and makes a few notes in my chart before turning back to me.

"There's not much swelling, but try to avoid walking on it as much as you can for the next few days. Keep it elevated and ice it a few times a day for twenty minutes each. Just give it a few days, and it will be good as new again."

"Thanks," I say, fixing my pant leg.

"Before you go, how's your head feeling?" he asks. He gets up from the rolling stool and gently feels my head.

"Fine," I say.

"No headaches, trouble sleeping, blackouts?"

"Nope."

He checks my eyes and ears. "Disorientation, nausea, or vomiting?"

"No, nothing like that. But I get a little dizzy sometimes."

"That's normal, but if it continues much longer, I'd like to see you back here." The doctor returns to his seat and makes a few more quick notes. "You are all set to go. Just take it easy for the next few days."

I hop down from the table, landing on my uninjured foot, keeping the other high enough from the ground to avoid jostling it. "Doctor, I know you said we could see Mom on Wednesday next week, but since we're here now, can I please see her? Just for a moment?" I clasp my hands and hold them to my chest, looking at the doctor with the best puppy dog eyes I can manage.

"Clarke—" Michelle starts.

"Pleeeeease?" I beg her, drawing out the *e* sound in the word.

They look at each other as if silently communicating. I wish I could read minds. But there's definitely something they don't want to tell me. I hold my breath, waiting for an answer. Then Dr. Underwood gives the briefest of nods to her before addressing me.

"She still has a few open wounds that haven't healed as much as I would like, but you can see her through the window. She only needs a few more days."

Michelle visibly relaxes. It's weird. I have no idea why Mom would need to be confined for her wounds. It's not like I wanted to lick her face or sneeze on her. But what do I know?

I narrow my eyes at him and wonder if he's human . . . or supe. If he is a supe, I doubt he'd go around advertising it. That thought makes me wonder. Mom is a witch, like Michelle and me. Could her quarantine have to do with some magic . . . something or other?

Those thoughts leave my mind as quick as they come, and all that remains is that I get to see Mom!

Michelle offers me her arm, and we follow the doctor out of the exam room and down the hall. I barely pay attention to where we are going, trying to walk fast and still avoid putting too much weight on one foot.

Not soon enough for my liking, we get to a hallway with several doors, each with their own large window looking in. Dr. Underwood stops in front of one room, and I limp closer, letting go of Michelle's arm. The tangy smell of copper fills my nose. I rub the back of my hand on my nose, trying to make it go away as I hop toward the window.

The window on the outside wall has the blinds drawn, but enough sunlight filters in, bathing the room in the warm glow of the late afternoon sun. Mom is sleeping. She looks pale, but peaceful.

I touch the glass, longing to hold her hand. But I'm just glad I can see her face. Even if her lips are pale and dry and cuts mar her face and arms. But I can see with my own eyes that she's healing. The steady rise and fall of her chest and the steady pulsing of the machine next to her both fill me with comfort. I can feel my stress ease quite a bit.

I'm not sure how long I stand there, but I know my good leg is starting to ache from supporting twice as much weight as normal.

A hot hand touches my arm, drawing my attention from Mom. "We should go soon, Clarke. The doctor has a lot of work to do." Then she turns to him and says, "Thank you for this. Seeing her helps."

"Not a problem."

I know he's busy, but still his voice is warm and friendly as if, standing here, watching me stare at Mom, is just as important as anything else. I look back toward Mom. There's so much I want to tell her, to ask her . . . I turn to the doctor, my hand still pressed against the cool glass. "When can I go in and see her?"

He checks her clipboard. "When you come back next Wednesday."

"Thank you," I say.

He smiles and gives one nod. "Of course."

I take a deep breath and let it out, and relief washes over me for the first time in three days.

CHAPTER 7

I flip through the list of shows and movies on the to-be-watched list I made three nights ago, after twisting my ankle, determined to stay in and binge a few shows. With doctor's instructions to ice my foot and stay off it as much as possible, I'm glad to take advantage of being stuck inside, where it's warm and decidedly not icy. After three days, though, it is beginning to wear on me.

We're going to visit Mom on Wednesday. I can't wait. Looking at the calendar pinned next to the door, I note it's been five days since I woke up. Only six more days until I can finally see Mom. It will be a late birthday present, but it's the only one I want or need. Maybe this time she'll be awake. If not, just being next to her will be enough.

The doctor told Michelle he would prefer we wait, just to give her time and peace to heal. It's still been hard. I understand their concern, but it still sucks. At least I got to see her through the glass window.

Michelle kisses me on the top of the head. "I'll be home early today to take you to the school to register for classes," she says as she heads out the door to work.

The day passes slowly, and I switch to reading when a headache starts to form after a little over an hour of watching TV, though I suppose it's been more like listening to it as I stare out the window, watching the barest amount of snow fall continuously. Between chapters, I doze for a few minutes here and there, then switch back to listening to the TV. I'm not used to being cooped up like this without being sick. It's terribly boring, and I still haven't managed to make it back to either of the bookstores yet.

It's a relief when Michelle comes home. I limp toward the bedroom, using the wall for support. My ankle doesn't feel too bad anymore, just a little stiff. And though I could probably walk without the limp, I don't want to push it. I tested it out last night and can move with a minimal amount of soreness. I don't want to be limping my way to class when I finally start school.

During the drive, a swarm of butterflies flutters in my stomach. After as many moves as I've been through, I shouldn't be feeling like this. I suppose it's the not knowing that gets to me. Each school was different. Some were great, others run of the mill, but then there were the terrible schools where bullies sought out the new kid and made my life hell.

I reach for my bag to get my wallet, and the strange scent of copper fills my nose. My wallet snaps into my open palm. I stare at my hand for a long moment. *What the crap was that?*

"Be careful." Michelle looks at me. "It's fine when it's just us. But you need to learn how to control your powers. They'll be erratic at first, but as long as you keep your emotions in check, you'll be fine." I blink, staring at her with my mouth open. She keeps talking like what I just did wasn't crazy. "And *never* do that in front of a human. Maybe I'll look into enrolling you in some classes to help you learn to control your powers."

"Okay . . ." is all I can manage to squeeze out. *More classes? I guess I'd better enjoy my down time while I have it. Doesn't seem like I'll be getting much over the next several months.*

"With the supermoon coming up on the nineteenth, you'll need to practice."

"Okay," I say again. I look at my hands and wonder what magic will feel like. Will it be mentally or physically taxing, or will it be easy —just have to will something to happen and . . . poof?

By the time we get to the school, my nerves are humming. I can feel my heart beating hard in my chest. Michelle waits for me to collect myself before we get out and walk up to the large brick building.

I follow behind Michelle as she leads me through the arched entryway and down the hall to an office with "Principal Friske" written across the glass door in bold, black lettering. She does most of the talking for me, but I make sure to introduce myself to the woman behind the desk and give her the best smile I can. It's strained, and I hope she doesn't take offense.

Michelle continues to talk with the woman behind the desk, and I excuse myself. "I want to check out my locker before we go, if that's okay."

"That's fine. I'll be waiting in the car whenever you're ready," she says, then goes back to talking. She's collecting a stack of papers. I nod, then close the door quietly behind me.

I exit the office and look around. Gray lockers line the halls, and I try to study the room numbers as I look at my schedule. I want to get a feel for the halls and the way the classrooms are numbered before I start. Nothing is worse than being late to every class because you have no idea where anything is. Or worse, get bad directions from a student who pretends to be helpful.

I make it to my locker just as the bell rings. The hall floods with students talking and lockers opening and slamming shut. A group of athletes passes, wearing their blue and silver letterman jackets. No one seems to notice me. Why would they? My face is about six inches from my locker. I stare at the locker combination in my hand and turn the dial.

It doesn't open. I double check the locker number, then try again, rolling my shoulders for good measure first. I take two deep breaths to push down my nerves and try again.

I reach for the dial and spin it a few times before attempting my combination again. It doesn't work. I frown, then look at the paper with my locker number to make sure I have the right one.

My face heats as I scoot over one locker. *Nope.* I look around and hope no one saw me. If they did, no one has said or done anything. I try again.

It opens, and I do a celebratory dance—on the inside. I breathe deeply.

The locker is clean and empty, but it will be full of books and school supplies soon. I close the door and turn the handle. When I turn around, Meghan pauses mid-stride.

"Clarke, you're here!" she says excitedly and gives me a brief hug.

"Yeah! I finally registered for classes. I start Tuesday."

"Oh, really? Can I see your schedule?" I pull the paper from my pocket and hand it to her. "Sweet, we have third and fifth periods together."

I can't help the inner sigh of relief. At least I'll see a friendly face in a few classes.

"That's great," I say.

Meghan shrugs her bag over her shoulder. "Well, I should get going. I have an afternoon shift to work today. But I'll see you next week."

"See you next week," I echo, waving as she takes off down the hall, her dark hair flowing behind her.

The crowd has thinned a lot now, so I head back the way I came, weaving through the few students taking their time. I earn a few curious stares from others, but so far, no intimidating glares. I'll take that as a win for now.

I head for a side door, toward the parking lot. Thankfully I don't run afoul of any more patches of ice and make it to the car in one piece.

"How does pizza sound to you?" Michelle asks as I slide into the car and buckle myself in. "I called in an order while I was waiting."

"Sounds fantastic!" I say. My stomach gurgles a little at just the thought.

She backs out of the parking spot and drives down Main Street, turning toward the town square. "Your mom's car will be ready tomorrow."

"Already? That was fast."

"We have some of the best mechanics here," Michelle says as she puts the car into park.

I wave my hand, stopping her from getting out. "Don't get out. I'll run in really quick and grab the food."

Michelle reaches into her purse and hands me some cash. "The order will be under my name."

I jump out and hurry inside, making my time in the rapidly chilling air as short as possible. There aren't many people here. It seems we managed to beat the dinner crowd.

It's a low-lit restaurant, with a comfortable atmosphere: booths made of dark-stained wood, the seats of worn leather, and red-and-white-checkered table cloths adorning the surfaces of the tables. The smell of garlic and tomato sauce fills the air, and I'm nearly drooling.

I hurry to the counter and bounce on my toes while I wait for the cashier to ring me up. I can't wait to get home and eat! He slides the pizza box to me—*large*—and I thank him as I turn away.

I can't help the small jig I do as I push the door open with my rear and step outside. The cold air blasts me in the face, and I can't help uttering, "Yuck."

By now it should feel familiar, expected even, but I'm still surprised when, as soon as I walk through the door, I'm jerked backward into a hard body. I nearly lose my grip on the pizza box.

Without looking, I know the chest at my back belongs to Seth. Ice falls and shatters at my feet. Exactly where I'd been standing. I blink and look around. I think I see a shadow pass by a tree, but when I blink again, it's gone. It was probably nothing.

"Why am I not surprised?" He lets me go, throwing his hands in the air as I spin to face him.

I open my mouth to say thanks, though what comes out instead is, "Why are you always around everywhere I go?"

"Not that it's any of your business, but I like to eat food on occasion. Is that all right with you?" he snaps.

Apparently, his snarky tone hit a nerve, because now I'm angry. "Why do you bother saving me if you hate me so much?"

41

Seth's eyes grow large. He looks taken aback, then after a moment, he says, "I don't hate you."

"Well, you obviously don't like me. And what I can't figure out is why you are nice to me one minute, and then the next, you act like you can't stand being in the same town." I wave my free arm around as I rant.

He takes my wrist and lowers my arm to my side, his other hand helping to steady the food in the other. "First, just put that away before you hurt someone." Seth pats me on my upper arm, like it'll go crazy and smack him—which I'm not entirely sure I wouldn't have if he hadn't pointed out my flailing. "Second, I'm sorry. I don't mean to be rude. It just worries me that someone can be so accident-prone and live to the ripe old age of . . ." He draws out the last word and raises his brows like he expects me to answer.

"Seventeen," I grunt.

"Seventeen. It's like you're always getting hurt or trying to get yourself killed. How did you even survive until now without a personal bodyguard?"

"I have never been accident-prone. This is just a coincidence," I say, pointing to the shattered ice at our feet. "Maybe you're just bad luck?" I try to keep a lightness to the jab, but he frowns. "Sorry," I mutter.

How can I chastise him for being rude when I'm rude as well?

"What about that first day?" I ask after what feels like several long moments. "You were rude then, and that was the first time I ever saw you."

He looks sheepish. "Sorry, you caught me on a bad day. I just got some . . . bad news."

There's something about the way he says *bad news* that keeps me from prying further. It sounds too personal, too painful. So I keep my lips pressed shut and twist the end of my ponytail around my finger.

He jerks his chin toward Michelle's running car. "I think someone is waiting on you."

"I-I should go," I say.

"I'll walk you to the car."

I don't even argue. I wouldn't win, even if I did. We walk the short distance in silence and without the anger or attitudes that have been present since I first bumped into him. I suddenly feel awkward around Seth.

I reach out for the door handle, and I feel his hand wrap around the top of the arm clutching the pizza. Only the fact that his gentle hold is steady is keeping me from the sin of dropping the box at my feet. His fingers are warm against my chilled skin even through my jacket. I turn slowly and look up at him. My heartbeat speeds up as he takes a step closer to me. The cold metal of the car presses against my back.

"Uh," he starts and seems to have trouble holding my gaze. "Let me make it up to you. Burger Bar has the best burgers you'll ever have."

Is he asking me out on a date? I scrunch up my nose. If he is, then I'm not sure. It might just be an apology. I think on that for a minute, stealing a glance at the pizza box, then say, "Tarantulas can go two years without eating."

Seth's eyes narrow slightly. "And are you a tarantula?" he asks teasingly.

I shake my head no.

"So . . . is that a yes?"

I lick my lips, nodding dumbly, and his smirk comes out to play across his face. My stomach flips, and it's not unpleasant. Seth leans forward and musses the top of my head playfully, then he turns and leaves, shaking his head and laughing softly to himself.

I look down at my hand to find a small slip of paper with a number written across it. *His* number. I feel heat rise to my cheeks as I climb into the car.

Wow . . . that was completely unexpected.

"What was that all about?" Michelle asks as I buckle myself in.

"I think . . ." Again, I look down at the slip in my hand. "I think I have a date."

CHAPTER 8

*H*olding my phone above me, I stare at the screen, rereading my message and debating if I should send the text or not. I roll over and hit send before I can talk myself out of it completely.

Clarke: hey, just texting so you have my number, too - Clarke

Lame . . . so lame. I smack the palm of my hand against my forehead. It could be worse, but it still feels cringeworthy. I am so *bad* at this stuff. Maybe I should have waited a few days—or a week, but now it's too late for what ifs. Though honestly, what would waiting prove? Waiting would have meant anxiety. And I already have more than enough of that to go around. Then there's the fact that he works for Michelle, so he already knows more about me than I know about him. I kind of want to even the score.

Seth: I didn't expect a text so soon

Crap. Double crap. I waited a day. I knew I should have taken longer before sending the text. Maybe I shouldn't have sent one at all. He probably thinks I'm some desperate loser now. Who would want to be friends with that?

Seth: You haven't changed your mind about going on a date with me, have you?

I swallow the ball of nerves working its way up my chest.

Clarke: It's a date?

Seth: What did you think it was?

Clarke: I don't know?

Seth: How does tomorrow sound? Around six?

Clarke: I guess I'll probably want to eat tomorrow

Seth: You're funny

Seth: Gotta run, something just came up

Seth: Pick you up at six?

Clarke: Okay

Seth: See you tomorrow

Clarke: Yeah. See you then

Two minutes later my phone dings with another message.

Seth: Good night, Clarke

I smile, then set my cell down on the nightstand and click off my light. When my head lands on my pillow, my eyes refuse to close. I will not be sleeping much tonight. I'm nervous about tomorrow, though I'm not sure why. It's not as though we haven't spent time together before.

But this was different. Those times were never intentional, and our conversations were mostly snarky. This feels weird. But in a good way.

CHAPTER 9

J sit on the couch nervously chewing on my thumbnail until I hear the rumble of a car outside. Jumping to my feet, I'm at the door, my hand hovering over the handle, waiting for him to knock.

I listen and hear his footsteps approach, then stop. He clears his throat. "Are you going to open the door?" Seth asks.

My eyes widen, but I stay quiet. This is already awkward, and we aren't even in the same room.

"I can see the top of your head through this little window." He taps gently on the glass pane right above my head.

Blowing out a breath, I pull open the door and motion for him to come in even though his car is still running. It's going to be nice and warm, which is good, because that blast of air that came in with him was enough to make me want to hibernate.

Seth smiles, and it's nice. One corner of his lips lifts a little higher than the other, showing off part of his eye tooth. There's something almost animalistic about the look. And it sends butterflies swarming in my gut.

I step away. "Shall we?"

He nods, and once I close the door behind us, he guides me to his car with one hand on my lower back. Part of me thinks it's because he's afraid I'll fall and break something, but another part wonders if he might be looking for an excuse to touch me.

Seth opens the car door for me, then closes it gently as I buckle myself in. The heat feels amazing, though as soon as he slides in next to me, I almost want to roll the window down, just a bit. Because with him so close, the heat is almost too much, as if the temperature went up twenty degrees the second he got in.

As if he can sense the overload I'm feeling, he reaches over and turns the dial down. I twist a strand of hair around my finger, again and again.

"It's okay," he says with a hint of laughter. "You can relax. I'm not going to bite."

There it is again, that smile that is both sweet and innocent, and dark and dangerous at the same time. The one that says he *could* bite if I wanted him to. I look away and out the side window, watching the town pass, trying to memorize where everything is. It only takes a few minutes to get to the restaurant.

He parks, and I look around. We're in Miller's Plaza. Daily Knead is straight ahead, and to our left is Burger Bar. I lick my lips. I scan the rest of the plaza, something I hadn't even bothered to do until now. Serendipity Dance Studio, VIP Nails, and . . .

"What is that place?" I ask, pointing.

Seth pauses halfway out of the car. His eyes travel in the direction I'm pointing.

"Sakura Buffet?" He gives me a strange look. "It's a Chinese, Vietnamese, and Japanese buffet. Why?"

I can feel my eyes growing large. I had given up all hope of there being a Japanese restaurant in this part of the country, but all three in one? I think I might be in heaven!

I get out of the car to find him still watching me with that look. Seth laughs lightly. "I was going to take you to Burger Bar, but we can save that for another day if you'd prefer to go to Sakura."

"Really?" I clasp my hands and can't help but do a body wiggle.

He laughs again, this time not bothering to try to suppress it. Seth walks around the car and offers me his arm. I take it, letting him lead me across the parking lot.

"If you like this place"—he gestures toward Sakura Buffet—"you'll *love* the Tacos for Daze food truck. I can take you there when it's warmer."

"Yes, please!"

We walk in, and the delicious smell of the food nearly knocks me over. I was too nervous to eat breakfast, so now I'm starving. My stomach lets out an embarrassingly loud growl.

"If you're not hungry . . ." Seth starts, a large grin plastered across his face.

"Don't even joke about food right now," I mutter.

There are twelve tables inside that would fit four people each and three booths along the large window facing out. The buffet is along the back, with a view of the kitchen behind it. In front of the buffet is the cashier.

I follow half a step behind him to the counter. While he gets the plates, I can't help but ogle the large variety of food. I am tempted to get a bite of everything. Glancing at the back of Seth's head, I frown. He might think I'm overly gluttonous. So I'd better stick to one or two things. But everything looks and smells so delicious.

We pick the booth along the window farthest from the door. I drop off my bag and drape my coat over it before heading to fill my plate.

I scan the buffet and am almost overwhelmed with the choices— chicken lo mein, boneless spare ribs, tempura shrimp, sashimi, and curry chicken! And so many more options. Ugh, how's a girl to choose?

I can always come back, I remind myself. So I settle on Kung Pao chicken with peanuts and a boneless spare rib. I load up my plate and head back to the table. A minute later, Seth joins me, somehow balancing two drinks in one hand and his plate in the other. He sits down next to me rather than across. I'm pinned between him and the wall, though I don't feel trapped.

We angle our bodies toward each other so we have a little more elbow room and chat between bites. He's easier to talk to than I expected. He has this way of asking me questions that don't feel invasive but have me revealing more about myself than I normally would to someone I just met. Seth's manner is relaxed. He's so different from the guy I met a week ago. Smiles come easy to him. And I want to know more about who he is.

Seth was right—the food here is really good. Before I know it, my plate is empty, and I'm tempted to go for another round. Instead, I pick up my drink and sip. He is watching me. More observant than most people, he almost seems like he's studying me. There's something not exactly human behind his gaze, and it makes me wonder . . .

Putting down the soda, I lean forward. He mirrors my movement, a conspiratorial smirk gracing his lips. I look around, and when I'm sure there is no one within hearing distance, I whisper, "What *are* you?"

I can tell that's not what he was expecting me to say. The grin slips from his face, and he looks half upset and half like I've grown a second head.

"What do you mean?" Seth asks slowly. His nostrils flare slightly.

It occurs to me then that he might just be another human. "Uh, I mean . . ." I stumble, looking for something to cover up my slip. "What's your sign?"

Oh. My. Gawd. I cringe visibly, and it's obvious he knows that isn't what I meant. Not even close.

He leans in a little closer and says, "Look, I will tell you this because I *know* your aunt." He puts an emphasis on *know*, as if it means more than *I'm her employee*. "You can't really go around asking people that here. There are people—humans—who don't know about supes, and there are some supes who would wish to remain unknown."

I struggle to get my tongue to form words. Of course it's rude to ask that. "Do you know what I am?"

He nods, slowly.

"How?"

He licks his lips. "I can smell the magic on you. It's faint, but it's there." I'm not even sure what that means. Seth leans back against the

ALI WINTERS

booth. "Besides, I do work for Michelle, and she already told me about your family."

I'm still leaning forward.

"So you know that I'm a—" I cut off. I don't know if I should say the word out loud. It's still unbelievable. After what happened in the car on the way to register for classes, I tried starting the fireplace for three hours straight. But nothing had happened, and I'd felt nothing.

"A witch?" he says in a normal speaking tone, though after whispering, it sounds more like shouting to my ears.

My eyes go wide, and I can feel a tingling in my chest, burning its way up my neck and scorching my cheeks. I can't believe he said it so loud!

"What are you doing?" I hiss.

"I'm just playing with you. Trust me, no one heard."

I cut my eyes to a man eating alone, with his back toward us only a few tables away. Seth just laughs. Of course, he's right. The man made no move to indicate he'd heard.

As soon as my heart climbs back down and out of my throat, I ask, "So, you know about me. Don't you think it's only fair for me to know about you?"

Maybe I'm imagining it, but I think he's a little embarrassed. "Shifter . . . wolf," he mumbles.

Finally, I lean back as well. I cross my arms and consider him, then I nod and say, "That explains a lot."

Seth cocks his head as if to tell me to go on.

"You do seem to growl an awful lot when you're annoyed," I clarify, eyeing him up and down.

He almost spits his drink out. Now it's my turn to laugh.

"No, I don't," he says defensively.

"I'm kidding," I say. "It's your eyes. They look almost golden in some light. It's not a very common eye color, and then . . . even when you hated me—"

"I never hated you," he says flatly and very seriously as he cuts me off.

I reach out and place one of my hands on top of his. "You still had a protective quality about you."

He says something, but I don't hear it. A ringing starts in my ears and grows louder and louder until I have to grasp the edge of the table to keep upright.

Seth grabs my arms and holds me up, talking to me, but the words are muffled and distorted by the ringing. I try to look up at him, and my eyes snag on a dark shape as it stands. I can't make out who or what it is. The lines are distorted, like bad reception on an old television set. I try to point it out to Seth, but I don't know if my words are coming out as more than gibberish or if they are only thoughts in my head.

Then the shadow is gone, and so is the ringing. I slump in my seat and try to catch my breath. My skin is like ice. The metal of my bracelet feels like it's burning in comparison.

"Clarke? Clarke!" Seth's worried voice breaks through my fog.

I snuggle closer to his warmth. This cold is nothing like the cold outside, but something deeper, something darker coating my bones.

"Clarke," he says again. More firmly this time.

I force myself to move, to straighten my spine, and look at him. Sharp pain pierces my temples. "I'm fine," I say weakly. "I just have a migraine."

His lips pinch together, and I know he doesn't believe me, but he won't argue here.

The drive home is silent. Thankfully my headache is mostly gone, only a residual pain remaining. And I'm so tired.

When Seth parks the car, he turns to me. At first I think he's angry, then I realize that's wrong. He's concerned.

"What happened back there?" His voice is soft, but the words are demanding.

I shake my head. "I don't know. I've been getting headaches a lot since I've been here. I don't think I've adjusted to the altitude yet, or maybe it's the concussion from the accident."

He considers me for a long moment and must believe that I'm not hiding anything, or at least not *trying* to hide anything. Though now, I think he might have a better idea of what's causing my headaches than I do.

I don't wait for him to open my car door, and by the time I get to the front of the car, he's at my side, linking his arm in mine as he walks me up the steps. Whatever bothered him about my dizzy spell seems to have dissipated.

I've never had a boy walk me to my door before. I've only seen things like that in movies, right before he kisses the girl. My pulse races.

"Clarke, I . . ." Seth takes his arm from mine and reaches into the pocket of his leather jacket. Then he's handing me a small dark blue box. My heart hammers as thoughts of what it could be and why he's giving it to me race through my mind.

I take it, running my fingers over the textured surface.

"It's nothing special, so don't read too much into it. It's more of a welcoming gift." He looks away, refusing to meet my eyes, and if I'm not mistaken, his face is a little flushed.

"Thank you," I say.

Before I can open it, he's running his hand over the top of my head. It's a strange gesture, almost brotherly. But it quickly changes into something more when his hand pauses at the nape of my neck, pulling me closer. I think he's going to kiss me.

He swallows hard, the knot on his throat bobbing. I lean forward into him. My hand rests on his chest, the other clutching the box at my side. Seth could melt snow with the heat that's radiating off him.

I try to control my breathing as our faces inch closer and closer.

And just when I can almost feel his lips on mine . . . Seth backs up and walks backward down the steps. "I'll talk to you later, Clarke. Feel better."

I am a little disappointed but also relieved. Because I think I might spontaneously combust if we kissed.

Clutching the box in my hand, I unlock the door and close it behind me. The sound of Seth's engine roaring to life doesn't come until I turn the lock on the front door.

CHAPTER 10

I slip off my boots and pad down the hall, pausing to say goodnight to the painting. There's just something about it that feels familiar. I squint at the man, and I swear he looks a little bigger than the last time again. Clearly that's impossible, so I laugh it off and continue to my room.

It's not until I shower and change into my nightclothes that I sit on the bed holding the blue box. There's something about prolonging opening up a gift that makes it even better. I lift the lid to reveal a glass ornament wolf. A gold string is looped through a hook in its back. It's beautiful. I set it next to the bedside lamp and pick up my cell.

Clarke: Thank you. I love it

Seth: I'm glad

Clarke: I'm sorry about tonight. I want to make it up to you

Seth: There's no need

Seth: You didn't do anything wrong

Clarke: Come to dinner tomorrow

I wait a few minutes, wondering if he even wants to, or if he'd only asked me out as a friend. But he'd said it was a date. And then there was that almost kiss. The longer he takes to respond, the more my mind wonders if I read him, and the date we had, all wrong.

Seth: So . . . is this a date? ;)

A large, almost painful grin spreads across my face at his response.

Clarke: Do you want it to be?

Even I'm surprised at my uncharacteristic confidence and ability to tease.

Seth: I look forward to it

My heart flutters in my chest. I click off the light, tuck myself under the blankets, and turn on my side to admire the wolf. The moonlight streams through my window, dancing through the cut glass facets and creating a beautiful rainbow of faded colors along the wall.

I look in the mirror and frown. Strip off the thick pink knit sweater and try on another. I really need to go shopping. Most of my clothes are too casual. The movers should have been here days ago with our things. We'll have to wait until Mom is home to find out what happened to them. At least the car arrived this morning, so now I have what was in my other suitcase in the trunk.

I sigh and go back to the first sweater I tried on, a thin knit the color of azure blue to match the sky.

There's a knock at the front door as I pull it over my head and smooth it down. I take a deep breath in and let it out, twice, before hurrying to the door. A glance at the clock tells me he's twenty minutes early.

Seth hurries inside as soon as the door opens, closing it quickly behind him against the wind and snow that blow in after.

"You look nice," he says, as if he's surprised to find that I did more than brush my hair.

"Thanks." We stand awkwardly for a moment. He's so close, I'm tempted to reach out and grab his shirt, pulling him even closer, to start where we left off last night. He quirks a brow, and one corner of his mouth ticks up, as if he knows what I'm thinking and knows I can't help it. I push the thought down until later, then add, "I still need to set the table. You can relax on the couch if you want."

Hurrying to the dining room, I put down the two plates and

napkins. I forgot to ask him what he wants to drink, so I just set down empty cups for now. I push my way through the swinging door into the kitchen and load up a tray with everything, then return to the dining room and set it down in the center. I take a second to make sure everything is straight.

"Okay, dinner is ready!" I call out to the other room and spin around when I hear laughing right behind me. "How long have you been standing there?"

"The whole time," he says. There's that arrogant smirk again.

"Sit down." I point to a chair with a jerk of my chin. He's looking from me to the food.

"What?" I ask.

"I don't know what I expected, but it wasn't tacos."

I gasp in mock horror, pressing a hand to my chest in melodramatic fashion. "It's your fault, you know. You were the one who mentioned Tacos for Daze."

Seth crosses the room, but instead of sitting down in one of the chairs, he stops less than a foot away. He lifts a hand and skims a lock of hair with one finger. "Tacos are great, but I really just came for the company."

Before I get a chance to attempt to formulate a response to that, the front door opens and slams quickly. "Clarke? Are you here?"

"In the dining room!" I call out.

It suddenly dawns on me that I invited him over without asking Michelle first. What is with me lately? I'm never this inconsiderate.

"Oh, Mr. Cooper, I didn't know you were coming over." Her eyebrows shoot up in surprise.

"I invited him over for dinner. I hope that's okay?"

She waves my concern away. "Oh, that's fine, dear." Her eyes graze the table then, before she walks into the kitchen. I can feel my eyes nearly bulge out of their sockets from the look she gives me. What does that woman *think* is actually going on here?

From the devilish grin on Seth's face, he knows exactly what Michelle is thinking. I make a slashing movement across my throat with my hand just as she returns with a pitcher of water.

"Why don't you join us?" I offer.

Michelle hesitates. "I don't want to intrude."

"We insist," Seth says.

"I'll go get an extra plate," I say, running off to the kitchen.

I stop on my way back to the dining room, my hand just shy of touching the swinging door when I hear them talking.

"You didn't need to come over to watch her tonight. She's been home all day. It's safe here," Michelle says.

Adrenaline spikes, and I am pissed. *Watch me? Watch me!* I'm not some helpless princess. And to ask me on a date to just—what? Keep an eye on me? The realization stings a lot more than I expect.

Who are these people, treating me as if I were a child? A minor slip on the ice isn't all that uncommon for someone not used to this kind of winter. It feels like a betrayal that Michelle had him follow me. No wonder he was there when I slipped. That's why he's always around.

"I don't mind, and this was—"

I don't wait to hear another word before I burst through the doorway. They both turn to face me, and from the look on their faces, they know I heard.

A tear falls down my cheek. *Traitorous body!*

"Who the hell do you think you are? I'm not—" My voice breaks. "You had him follow me, watching me? I'm not some invalid incapable of taking care of myself!"

They both stand at the same time. Seth takes one step forward, hand reaching out for me.

"Sweetie, it's not like that—" Michelle starts, but I don't let her finish before I round on Seth.

"And you . . ." I seethe. "How could you? I don't need or want your pity dates!" I'm shaking now. Rage races through me in an icy wave. I'm crying, and I don't care anymore. "You made me think you liked me."

He recoils like I slapped him. "Clarke, please just listen. It's not—"

"No. Just get out and leave me alone."

I turn on my heel and storm off before either of them have a chance to say another word, before they have a chance to make up some lie to try to make me feel better, to try to justify having him follow me. I slam the door to my room behind me.

A few minutes later, the front door opens and shuts, and I wait for the roar of his car's engine, but there's only silence.

I've never felt more alone in my life than I do now.

CHAPTER 11

*A*n annoying buzz drags me from sleep, and I peel my eyes open. They feel swollen from crying. I groan and roll over to my side.

The glass wolf is staring at me from the night stand as if pleading with me to listen to Seth. *Fat chance.* I don't want to hear what he or Michelle has to say. I feel betrayed, like I'm the butt of some twisted prank. I avoided them both all day yesterday. I just can't see myself being ready to talk to them yet.

I glance at the calendar. Tomorrow is the nineteenth, so I'll at least get to see Mom in two more days.

My phone buzzes again. I pick it up and glare at the name across the display. Seth. I hit ignore and place it face down. I can't believe I wanted to kiss that jerk, *almost* kissed him. And just as I promised myself I wouldn't do, I was rushing into something. Letting my heart lead the way instead of my brain.

Throwing my covers off, I get up and move into the living room to watch whatever happens to be on TV, flipping blindly through the channels.

The vibration of the cell on the wood surface echoes down the hall, so I turn up the volume to drown it out.

"Take a hint," I mutter.

Though I lay on the couch with my eyes pointed at the screen for several hours, I don't remember a minute of anything I've "watched." I've played what happened last night over and over in my head, wishing they'd tried saying something different, wishing they'd tried to give me something better than excuses . . . wishing I'd said more to let them know that what they did was horrible. But alas, I don't have the skills required for time travel.

My stomach growls loudly, and I realize it's already the middle of the afternoon, and I haven't eaten yet. Maybe walking to the burger joint will help clear my head.

Standing inside the doorway to my room, I listen for the vibration of my phone. Thankfully, it's silent. I quickly throw on a pair of leggings and an oversized faded red sweater that clings to my form. I wonder what kind of shopping this town has and if I'll have to go to the next town over to have a selection.

For a brief moment, I debate taking the car. It would be warm for sure, but I think I need the exercise to clear my head. And it doesn't seem too chilly out today. The fact that I'd rather face the cold than use a nice warm car doesn't escape me.

As I finish slipping on the knee-high boots, my phone buzzes. My stomach forms into a knot. That's it. I am not going to walk there and back with the constant buzzing. I just want a few hours of peace. For a moment, I'm tempted to look at the number of missed calls and messages, though that passes quickly.

Instead, I march out of my room, snatching up my jacket on the way out, pausing to grab the house key—now attached to our car keys —from the bowl next to the door. I pause at the bottom of the steps and look back at the townhouse, wondering if I *should* bring my phone after all. No, if I get lost, I'll just ask someone for directions. I'll be home long before Michelle.

The sun shines, and I'm glad for its warmth, but the glint off the snow is nearly blinding. I look around me as I walk. The birds sing, and as I focus on their song, I find my muscles release their tension. It's peaceful, and more beautiful than I gave the town credit for, with the snow-covered pines and the mountains in every direction.

By the time I reach Burger Bar, a super cute drive-in straight out of the fifties, I've warmed up. It's right across from my future school and in front of the plaza where the Daily Knead is.

I knew Burger Bar looked retro from the outside, but inside is a whole other level of epic. Black-and-white-checkered flooring, with just enough wear and tear that I know it's original. Booths with the classic red-and-white leather, stools at the counter to match. Polished tin ceiling tiles. I haven't seen anything like that since Mom took me to Salem, Massachusetts, when I was twelve. There is definitely some history to this place. The only thing that doesn't quite fit is the TV in the back.

I sit down at a table to peruse the menu. I quickly settle on a cheeseburger and fries. It's always been my belief that you can tell a lot about a place by how well it does the basics. It doesn't take long for me to shed my jacket. After being out in the crisp air, I'm a little warm.

The Beatles play from a jukebox, and I tap a finger on the metal table while I wait for my food. Staring blankly out the window, I let my mind wander. My eyelids grow heavy as I sit alone at this little table, content and surrounded by the scent of delicious food. My mouth waters, and my stomach growls loudly in response. I must be hungrier than I realized.

I hear a chuckle, warm and inviting enough to send a tingle along my skin. My spine straightens as a knot forms in my chest. Slowly, I turn and look over my shoulder. My heart stutters, and I struggle to breathe as two amber eyes lock onto mine.

Seth takes a few steps toward me and hesitates when I shake my head, but continues to approach regardless. I command my body to move, though it ignores me and stays right where it is.

I feel like a caged animal.

Trapped.

I stand, ready to bolt.

"Wait, please," Seth says quietly. The tips of his fingers rest on my wrist. I curse how much I want to sink into his touch.

There's something in his eyes that makes me want to sit back down. Something that looks so sincere, almost so heartbreaking it makes my knees weak.

"What?" I ask through clenched teeth. I don't want him to know how I feel. It's stupid, but I don't care. There's still too much hurt, and it hasn't even been a full day yet.

"Please sit," he says, and when I don't, he adds, "Give me two minutes, and then you can leave, or I'll leave. I won't bother you again."

I don't know what I want. Do I never want to see him again, or just not for a while? I haven't thought that far ahead. Neither option is ideal. What I *want* is for him to have not played errand boy for my aunt, for him to not pretend to like me because it makes keeping an eye on me easier for him.

So I sit and agree to give him two minutes.

Seth's shoulders slump, and he lets out a breath. "I'm sorry, Clarke. I should have told you the first time."

"Yes, you should have," I snap. Crossing my arms, I avert my gaze, glaring at the floor. "You made me think you liked me," I say, the words almost too quiet.

He reaches out until his fingers brush the material of my sleeve, then he withdraws, curling his fingers into his palm. "That wasn't an act. I really do like you."

I want to believe him. My heart speeds up, happy to hear his words, but my brain is shouting *idiot,* and telling me not to listen to the lies. Grudgingly, I meet his eyes, though I stay silent.

"I really am sorry." His brows pull together. "Michelle only asked me to keep an eye out for you *if* I saw you. That's all. She didn't ask me to follow you. She was just worried."

"But you did follow me?"

"No, that was all a coincidence." Seth slashes a finger in an X motion over his heart. "Promise."

"But she said you didn't need to watch me last night, like you were supposed to watch me some other times," I insist.

"I think when she saw me at the house, she assumed I

misunderstood what she'd asked and why I was really there." Now he reaches out and takes my hand in both of his.

"And why were you there?"

He looks at me with a rueful smile. "For you. To spend time with you. I never told her I'd asked you out on a date. I don't think she even knew I liked you. She knows now."

"Oh." Well, that certainly gives me plenty to think about. I did only hear her say he didn't need to watch me, and I don't actually know what he'd been planning to say when I walked in on their conversation. He could be lying now, but I don't believe he is. There's something so sincere in his expression and in the way he spoke. Michelle isn't a bad person, and I doubt she'd hire someone who was underhanded.

Seth lets my hand slide out of his grasp and onto the table. It's cold in comparison to the heat of his hands. Then he gets up and turns. And I know what I want.

"Wait." It comes out louder than I intend. "You can stay."

When he faces me, I smile nervously. "Are . . . you sure?" he asks.

"Have lunch with me, my treat."

He scoffs lightly and sits down just as my food comes. He orders a strawberry shake, which doesn't take long to arrive.

It's awkward between us, though I'd rather have that any day than avoid him. I hate being upset with people. It sends my anxiety through the roof. I eat my fries from the basket and debate how to tackle the massive cheeseburger next to them while he drinks his shake. Neither of us say anything for a long time, and I can feel the awkwardness grow thicker by the second until I'm practically squirming in my seat.

"Strawberries aren't actually berries," I say between bites of fries when the silence becomes too much to take any longer.

"Oh? What are they then?" Seth snatches a couple fries and downs them before I can protest.

I take a sip of my Coke. *Fine. I can share.*

"They are still a fruit but not a berry, since berries have their seeds on the inside." I take a huge bite of my burger and have to consciously stop myself from moaning out loud. *Holy fish sticks, Batman, that is good.*

Seth laughs, though I can't tell if it's my weird knowledge of strawberries or the face I must be making.

He raises a hand and waves at someone over my head. I turn to look and see a girl with long golden brown hair standing next to a very tall guy with dark brown hair, both waving back. They approach the table, and I hurry and set my burger back down in the basket while I try to finish my bite before they reach us. I wipe my hands on my napkin.

"Eris, Rylan, what are you two doing here?" Seth asks in a cheerful voice. I can tell by the way the three of them regard each other that they have a close bond.

"Not much, just grabbing a bite to eat," Rylan answers.

The girl, Eris, smiles at me, her honey-colored eyes sparkling. She's a little taller than me, but much more athletic. She reaches a hand out toward me. "Eris Blaekthorn."

Her grip is firm.

"Clarke Price," I say, feeling a bit awkward.

Rylan shakes my hand next, and we exchange pleasantries. He's even larger close up. I see what I think is the corner of a tattoo peeking out from the hoodie he's wearing. Seth and Rylan immediately fall into a conversation. So I turn my attention back toward Eris. She's wearing minimal makeup, but it brings out her natural beauty.

"You're new here, right?" Eris asks.

I nod. "Yeah, I'll be starting Havenwood Falls High Tuesday."

"Great! I'll probably see you around. Look for me during lunch."

"I will," I say.

"Well, we should get going. See you around, Seth," Rylan says. They turn and head to a less crowded area.

Seth settles back in his chair. "Eris is a senior, so you might have a few classes with her," he explains.

I jerk my chin toward them. "Isn't he in school?" I ask, wondering why Seth would assume I'd only have classes with one of them.

"No, he graduated last year." Seth helps himself to another fry.

I take a bite of my burger. That makes sense.

"Eris is the daughter of my alpha," he adds in a little quieter tone.

I nearly choke on the food in my mouth and peer over my shoulder. Eris waves at us from across the restaurant. "What about him?"

"Same as me. Sentinel and hunter."

"Oh" is all I can think of to say, so I stuff my mouth full of fries. Though she's soft-spoken, there is something about Eris I can't put my finger on that makes her command attention when she speaks. I hadn't even thought about the possibility of a pack for shifters, but I suppose it makes sense.

I'm only half finished with my food when he looks at his watch. "I have to run to work. I didn't realize how late it got."

I'm disappointed that he has to leave. Seth pulls out his wallet, but I shake my head and try to swallow my bite as fast as possible. "I said it was my treat."

He smirks as if he's trying to be good-natured, but I can see he doesn't like that I'm buying him a shake. I barely hold back the urge to roll my eyes at his well-meaning but dated view on food. Then his eyes sparkle mischievously. "Fine, but only if you let me take you out again. Soon."

"Okay." I can't stop the smile that forms across my lips. I've forgiven him completely. And it only took two minutes—maybe less —and a strawberry shake. It might be a mistake, and as many times as I tell myself to keep my heart guarded, I fail to listen. The risk will either pay off, or someday I'll learn. Maybe. Probably.

He leaves, and I find sitting alone no longer feels as peaceful, now that it's tainted by the touch of loneliness. The afternoon has ended with me feeling completely different than how I started the day. I hurry and finish my food, ready to go home. I think I need to talk to Michelle as soon as she comes home. I'd like to clear the air.

After paying, I bundle back up and head out the door, holding it open for an older man who's coming in for a late lunch. His shoulder bumps mine, and I am knocked slightly off balance, but manage to catch myself.

"Excuse me, miss," he says at the same time as the automatic sorry leaves my mouth.

My heart thumps hard against my chest once. He looks familiar, though I can't place where I would know him from. He probably just has one of those faces.

And then he looks back at me, his voice dark when he says, "You should stay away from that one." His head jerks toward the table where Seth and I were sitting. "Bad things will happen if you continue to let him cling to you."

Cling? Bad things? I frown, not understanding this stranger. Is Seth into something I don't want to know about? Who is this old man? My vision tilts for a few seconds, and when it settles again, the man is already inside. I twist the bracelet around my wrist a few times. He probably thought I was someone else.

When I make it home, I pull my keys from my pocket and unlock the door as I stomp the snow from my boots. The cold combined with my now full belly have made me sleepy.

A yawn rips itself from me as I drop the keys in the bowl next to the door. My boots are soaked, so I toe them off, too lazy to bend over and remove them by hand. It takes me a few tries, but if I sit down to remove them, I won't be getting up anytime soon.

Maybe a little nap would be nice. I glance at the painting as I move down the hall. The man standing in the forest has both hands in the air. Now, I *know* he wasn't doing that before. Either I've gone insane or my memory for detail is worse than I thought. Because paintings don't move. And anyone who thinks they do would have to be certifiable.

Tired. I am definitely tired if I'm this confused over a painting.

CHAPTER 12

I run. The forest flies by in a blur as I struggle to catch my
breath. I'm barefoot and only wearing my flannel night
pants and my worn Tea-Rex shirt. Snow has matted my hair to my
head. It's cold, but I don't seem to feel it through the sickening panic
coursing through my veins.

I don't know how I got here. I don't even know where *here* is.

But I can't stop. Something is chasing me. I can hear it crashing
through the branches, its feet crunching against the snow, drawing
closer and closer behind me. Its panting and snarling grow louder.

My aunt's house looms up ahead, and I push my body faster,
though I'm not sure my legs can keep up this pace for much longer.
What is happening?

I can see someone standing on the porch. I open my mouth to call
out, but my lungs are struggling as it is. *Almost . . . there . . .*

I slip in the mud at the foot of the stairs, and I can feel the shadow
of whatever is chasing me crash down. Too close. Somehow, I manage
to scramble up the steps, and Michelle pulls me inside and slams the
door.

She's asking me what happened. I know this because I read her
lips, but I can't hear anything other than the ringing in my ears. Then

my body crumples to the ground, and darkness consumes my consciousness.

I sit up, panting. A dream. It was only a dream, even though it felt so real.

Letting out a loud breath, I fall back onto my pillows.

Dim light filters through my window. I look to the alarm clock. It's barely five a.m. It's way too early to get up on my first day at a new school, but after that nightmare, I don't think I could fall back asleep. When my heart rate slows enough that I know it won't explode, I get up and walk down the hall. The hardwood floor almost feels warm under my cold feet.

Michelle is in the kitchen, making jam. Does this woman even sleep? She looks like she's been up for hours.

The sugary sweetness fills the air. She stops humming and looks up, startled to see me standing there. I appreciate that she gave me space and didn't try to force me to listen. I didn't even hear her come home last night.

"I'm sorry about the other night," I blurt out. "Seth told me everything. I should have listened to you and not just assumed the worst."

Michelle smiles and continues to pour red mush into mason jars. "Don't worry about it, dear. It was a miscommunication on all our parts. Let's just forget all about it."

I wonder if her willingness to brush it off is because in her mind it isn't a big deal, or because we still don't know each other all that well and she doesn't want to do anything that might be seen as taking my mom's place. But if she's okay with letting it go, then so am I. Besides, now that I'm up early, it's the perfect chance to talk to her about this witchy stuff.

"Sounds good to me," I say, walking to the cabinet to get a bowl. I snatch the box of cereal from the top of the fridge on my way to the table and pour myself a big bowl.

I step on something dry and crusty. Moving to the side, I look down. It seems to be a small bit of dried mud. My vision wavers as I try to examine it, and I stumble. A shower of rainbow colored flakes scatter around me. I shake my head, falling to my knees to clean up the mess. "I'm sorry!"

"Clarke? Are you all right?" She stoops to place a hand on my shoulder.

"Yeah, just dizzy. I think I slept too long."

Michelle lifts me by my arms and tells me to sit in the wooden chair at the table while she sweeps up. I feel bad letting her take care of my mess, but if I'm being honest, my legs feel a little too unsteady right now.

"Has this happened before? Do you need to see the doctor?" She asks this casually, but the lines around her mouth are drawn tight. Michelle brings a broom to where I spilled.

"No." I wave my hands. "No, it's nothing like that. I want to say it's something else. But it's hard to explain. I just feel overwhelmed when it happens. It's probably just because I fell asleep so early."

She's quiet for a while as she finishes sweeping up the cereal. "Is it a surge of energy one second, then a drain the next?"

I nod that it is.

"I thought so," she says. She places the broom and dustpan back where they belong, then leans against the counter. "Your powers are starting to come in. Being so close to your birthday, that is to be expected. If you don't know what to expect, they can catch you off guard." She walks over, pulling out a chair and sitting a few inches in front of me. "I'm going to call the school, and tell them you'll be starting on Wednesday instead."

"No," I start to protest. Starting in the middle of the week is the worst.

"I insist. I don't want you fainting from these surges and getting hurt. It's only one more days."

After the wave I experienced, I know it would be safer to wait, especially after and being told these episodes would continue to get stronger until my powers fully come in. Though I've been looking forward to seeing Meghan again, and maybe getting to know Eris a little more, but they'll still be there later this week.

"What will it be like?" I ask when Michelle gets off the phone. I keep telling myself to think about it, to talk to Michelle about it, but it's just not something I want to face, not for longer than a few seconds at a time, anyway. It feels like a fantasy, and it's too much with everything else—the accident, the new town, and Mom still in the hospital.

"You will feel it more than most because the supermoon will enhance your magic tenfold. For most of us, though, we hardly notice it."

This doesn't make me feel good. I almost feel like a freak, even among my own family. "But what will happen?"

"It's different for everyone. It all depends on how *you* feel about it, how open you are, and of course, the strength of your powers. You will be the most powerful Price woman in generations." Michelle says this like it's something to be proud of, or excited about.

"Is it like this for every witch?"

"No. Most witches are born with their powers. Our line doesn't develop them until our eighteenth birthday."

I frown. "Why?"

Michelle shrugs. "For as long as I know of, even further back when our family first moved to Salem—"

"Salem?" I blurt. "You mean we were Salem witches?" I've always found that part of history fascinating, if not terrifying and heartbreaking. But to know my family had been there . . . I'd always thought my family was from the Northwest. I was way off!

"Yes, our family line has always been dependent on the moon. Strongest during the full moon, and weakest during the new moon. However, the sect of lunar witches our family comes from is small. Like the majority of witches in Havenwood Falls, most are born with their powers."

Then something strikes me as strange. "So why haven't I ever seen Mom do any kind of magic?"

"Angela was born with her powers, raised right here in Havenwood Falls, where she met Mason. When she was young, she chose to wear an amulet to suppress her powers. She had dreams of traveling the world and didn't want to feel dependent on them. And when Mason disappeared . . ." She trailed off.

"Who's Mason?" I ask slowly, though deep down I am pretty sure I already know.

"Mason was my brother . . . and your father."

"My father?" I think my mind is imploding. *My father!* "Do you know where he is?"

Michelle shakes her head. "No. No one has seen him since that night."

I knew my mother had me right after high school, but she's never spoken of my dad. He was gone before I was born. Maybe he isn't the deadbeat I've always assumed he was. Or maybe he is. For all I know, he took that opportunity to run and avoid the responsibility of a kid straight out of high school. I came into this conversation with a handful of questions, but now a million more pop up in their place.

"This just feels so crazy. I feel like I'm losing my mind. Stuff like this only happens in movies or books, not in real life."

She pats my hand, and I think she means it to be comforting. "I know, dear. But it *is* real. This is why you and your mother moved here, and . . ." She trails off. Michelle's eyes cloud over, and she stands abruptly and goes back to pouring jam as if we'd been talking about the weather.

There was something else. Something she started to say that she doesn't want me to know. A spark of annoyance flickers in my gut. I understand that she cares about me and wants to protect me, but it doesn't excuse deciding what I can and can't handle or keeping things from me.

"And what? What aren't you telling me?" I stand.

Michelle sets down her jar and wipes her hands on a dish cloth. Her chin drops to her chest as if the towel she's using is the most interesting thing in the world. Her body is turned away, and the light through the window silhouettes her profile. "Your father's twin, Tamsin. Your mother called me saying she'd felt his presence last month and was worried for you. We both decided that it would be safest to bring you here. She knew I could protect you in Havenwood Falls."

"How do you know?" I have an uncle I've never heard of before. Normally, I think that finding more family would be a good thing. Why would Mom and Michelle fear him? The thought of someone related to me being a danger makes me feel sick. I wrap my arms around my middle.

"There are wards around Havenwood Falls. Any resident gone longer than a month starts to forget about it, and visitors forget immediately. And he's never been here." She raises her brows. "Haven't you ever wondered why your mother needed to take monthly trips for work?"

I hadn't. I just assumed she had particular clients. "So what does this have to do with my uncle?"

Michelle walks over to me and grips my shoulders with her hands. She is stronger than she looks. "He wants to take your powers."

"I don't understand," I say. He's my uncle. Why would he want to take something from me?

"Your uncle turned to black magic when his powers never developed to the same strength as the rest of us. He tried to kill your father and take his powers, but our sister, Sarah, got in the way. She died protecting Mason that night."

What if my uncle did something to my dad?

My eyes go to the spot on the floor where I thought I'd seen the mud. It's gone now. I don't think I saw her scrape it up, and I don't know if Michelle would have said anything to me about tracking dirt inside.

I don't know what else to say. Michelle doesn't seem to know either, so I excuse myself and curl up on the couch, covering myself with a thick faux fur blanket, and stare out the window, trying to process everything. I think I'd almost prefer to be insane than face the fact that all of this might actually be very real.

CHAPTER 13

I yawn and stretch the seatbelt away from my neck as I let my head lull to the side. The falling snow streaking by in the dark, lit by the headlights of our car, is hypnotizing.

My body grows heavy, and my breathing slows. I think I've been here before. Some cheery song from decades before I was born plays on the radio softy in the background. Mom is humming along, her hands quietly tapping along to the beat of the music on the steering wheel.

We've been driving since long before the sun rose. I don't know why we couldn't make this a two-day trip. But it's been nearly a full day of nonstop driving.

I already miss my home, my school, and the few friends I had. The farther we go, the more I can feel the distance grow between me and the small town of Boring, Oregon—which really isn't as boring as the name suggests. It was actually named after the city founders.

I pull my jacket over my lap and use it as a blanket. Even with the heat on, the cold seeps in through the glass of the windows.

My eyes droop, half closing as I struggle to stay awake. I watch the headlights skim along the winding road.

I blink, and there's a dark shape ahead in the middle of the road. A shadow the light cannot penetrate. I blink again. Then my eyes widen as my entire body lurches forward. Mom swears and slams on the brakes.

Screeching fills the air, drowning out my mom's shouts . . . and I think my screams as well.

Time slows for a single heartbeat, and I can see the shadow—a man. His face remains shrouded in darkness. He lifts his arm, then my world is in chaos. The car skids on ice, flipping over and over.

There's a loud crack, then I feel a sharp pain in my head and damp warmth. When the world stops again, I am upside down. I reach to undo my seatbelt and free myself, but I can't lift my arms. I'm too tired, and everything hurts too much. The darkness is rushing in, swallowing up the light of our headlights against the snow.

I blink. And I hear sirens. I try to keep my eyes open, but I think I'm fading in and out because the next things I see are blue-and-red flashing lights. Then strange voices surround us. I try to speak, to call out for help. I don't know if my voice is broken from screaming or if my mouth didn't even open.

Rough hands are grabbing me. Gravity pulls on me, and I'm lifted into the air.

Then the dark comes again.

I gasp for breath as if I haven't been breathing for a while. It's painful. My body jerks up, and there is nothing but silence everywhere.

It wasn't an accident after all.

I'm sitting in the middle of the forest floor. Snow falls everywhere, except on me. When I look down, my hands are covered in something dark. At first I think it's mud, but it's warm and sticky. *Blood*, I realize.

I strain my ears, listening for the slightest clue to where I am.

A branch snaps behind me, and a shout echoes through the trees. Another voice joins the first. Two men are arguing, I think. I get up and run toward them. Fronds reach out like arms, trying to hold me back, roots and uneven ground working to trip me, to slow me. But I push on until I reach the edge of a clearing.

I can't make out their faces, but they have their hands on each other, as if almost to the point of striking, but holding back for some unknown reason. One shoves the other, forcing him to stumble away to avoid falling. He doesn't stay back for long. In two long strides, he runs and jumps. His body flies through the air, and he transforms into a . . . wolf.

It's so unexpected, I stagger, tripping over a tangled vine or some other plant. I don't take my eyes from the two men.

The other man is lifting his arm. Moonlight catches his face, and I know him now. He is the man in the street, from when Mom and I crashed. And he's the same man I've seen around town. The younger one in the town square, the homeless man, the old man from Burger Bar—he was always the same.

At the time, I thought they were all different, their ages impossibly too far apart. But now as I remember them, the veil of whatever had made me see differently has lifted, and my memories are crystal clear.

The wolf lunges. Something dark and sharp flies from the man's hand, striking the wolf through its massive neck.

It falls to the ground, dead.

I scream.

My eyes fly open. I'm breathing hard, drenched in sweat, and tangled in my covers. Another dream? I don't understand them, but I know deep down that they mean something. The soft light of predawn is breaking through the window. I don't think I can get back to sleep now, even if I wanted to.

Dropping my feet off the edge of the bed, I look over to see the glass wolf is knocked over. I reach out and set it back up. I must have hit the nightstand in my sleep during that awful nightmare.

My phone dings. Picking it up, I check the display and see Seth's name across the top.

Seth: I know you're sleeping, but do you want to come over and watch a movie after school?

The haunting feeling of my dream lingers and pushes down on my heart, squeezing it. I know what I want to say, but do I dare? The man from my dream, the one who'd warned me to stay away from Seth— what if he wasn't crazy after all? What if the warning he gave me to stay away from Seth wasn't a warning . . . but a threat?

I quickly type my response, then silence my phone, setting it face down on the nightstand. Tears sting my eyes, and I make my way into the bathroom, turning the shower on as hot as I can stand.

Seth is the first guy I've really liked since my ex, Jordan, broke up with me a year and a half ago. But if my dream really was a warning, and I continued to see Seth . . . I would never forgive myself if something happened to him.

As the hot water rains down over me, I lean my back against the cold porcelain wall and cry.

CHAPTER 14

I make my way out to the living room. My days are starting to bore me, and I can't wait until tomorrow, when I can finally start school and talk to Mom. I've already read the few books I brought with me, and I'm bored of all the TV shows. I should make an effort to get to the bookstore in town soon.

There's a pink envelope sitting on the coffee table with my name on it. I open it and read the card inside. In Michelle's neat handwriting is a note that reads:

Happy birthday! Relax and sleep in. We'll celebrate tonight when I get home. I shouldn't be any later than three.

P.S. Give Seth a call and see if he'd like to join us for dinner.

Today is my birthday, and I didn't even realize it. The smile on my face falls when I read his name. I want to invite him, but I can't take that chance. That dream was way too real.

Still, I go back to my room and grab my favorite book to reread. Pausing in the doorway, I regard my cell, then snatch it up, taking it with me. I'm not mad at him, though this would be so much easier if I was.

I trot back out into the living room and huddle on the couch. A few texts from him have already come in.

Seth: If you can't, that's okay. But why don't you want to see me anymore? Is it something I did?

Seth: I thought things were okay?

Seth: Clarke? Tell me what happened.

I read his messages, but I don't respond. Instead, I curl up on the plush white couch, draping a blanket over my legs, and open my book. My phone is tucked between my side and the couch. After one or two more messages, it goes quiet.

It's snowing, which makes the world feel like a sleepy, quiet place. Like I'm the only one around within miles. I stare into the snowy morning outside, admiring the beauty as the sun finishes rising, while I get to stay inside, warm. Then I get lost in my book.

A few hours later, a buzz against my side jolts me, and I nearly jump up. Letting out a quick breath, I check my phone.

Seth: I don't know what's going on but please talk to me.

Seth: Don't shut me out.

Seth: Do you need help? Are you in trouble? Your text has me worried.

I should message him back. My fingers hover over the screen for a long moment before I push the side button and darken the display. I *want* to respond. I just don't know what to say. I doubt "My dream and some crazy old guy told me to stay away or you'll get hurt" would suffice. Even I wouldn't believe that, and it was my dream, my experience.

Casually I drop the phone to the far side of the couch and go back to reading. I don't know how long it's been when the sound of a loud engine breaks my concentration. I look up to see Seth's dark blue car pulling around the corner, headed for my driveway.

I dash off the couch and run to the front door, making sure it's locked. His footsteps are heavy with snow as he walks up the few steps. I press my back against the door and crouch down. He knocks and calls out to me.

If I let him in now, I know my resolve to avoid him will break. But it's so tempting to give in. He sounds worried. I just don't think I can risk it.

"Clarke? Please talk to me. You don't even have to let me in. Just let me know you're okay."

I clench my fists on top of my knees to keep from reaching up and unlocking the door.

"Please. I know you're home."

I hear him sigh. I wait two beats, three . . . four. Then I can't take it anymore, and I start to straighten my legs. But now he's turned and is walking back to his car. I lift myself up on my toes and peek out the small glass window at the top of the door in time to see him pull away.

My stomach turns leaden. I need to talk to Michelle. I need to find some way to make it so he's not in danger just from knowing me. My mind flashes back to the glass wolf knocked over and to the dream with the wolf leaping and being struck down. I've never believed in omens before, but I know those two things combined are some kind of warning. Something in my gut is telling me to listen to the signs.

I go back to the couch and read until my stomach growls. I look out the window; the sun is already starting to set. I know it's winter, and sunset comes early, but Michelle should be home by now. I bend over, picking my phone up from the ground, and look at my missed messages.

There's nothing. Michelle must have lost track of time at work. I can't help but feel disappointed. It's her business, and I get that. As far as I know, she only has a handful of people working for her—Seth, Meghan, and a few others. But loneliness still creeps in.

I wish Mom was out of the hospital. I just want to see her. I want her to tell me everything will be okay. I just need to be in the same space as her. To talk to her, even for a few minutes.

I suppose I could drive to the bakery, but then Seth might be there. And if I see him, I know I'll spill everything, even if it makes me sound like a crazy person.

No, I'll just wait until Michelle comes home.

There's a clatter of metal, and my head jerks up. My book falls to the floor. I rub my forehead. I must have fallen asleep reading. The sky is pitch black against the bright supermoon drowning out the stars just over the edge of the horizon. The light reflects off the snow, making the night feel eerie. The tire tracks from Seth's car have faded a little, so I know it snowed an inch or two while I slept. My aunt's car isn't outside.

I rub my eyes, then do an inventory of how I feel. Michelle said my powers would come in tonight. But I feel the same as I have every other day of my life. Should I be able to feel them? Doesn't matter. I will ask her about it in the morning.

I check my phone. No new messages. It's late, almost ten. She has to be home. So I walk quietly toward her bedroom. She must have come in and seen me sleeping and just let me be. I shiver. She might have parked on the side of the house.

The door to her room is open, and her bed remains untouched. There's not a single light on in the house.

The sound comes again, and if I'm not mistaken, it sounds like something knocked the lid off the garbage can outside. Probably just a raccoon. I should pick it up so Michelle doesn't have to deal with it after her long day.

I don't know if Michelle has to work tomorrow, but I bet she's barely going to get any sleep tonight. She's never up this late, let alone at work past six. I yawn and pull on my jacket and boots.

Wow. I didn't even get out of my nightclothes today. Talk about a lazy day. I'd be embarrassed, but other than Seth knocking on the door, I haven't been around another person all day. *Happy birthday to me.*

I grab my phone and stuff it in my flannel pants pocket in case I need a flashlight and unlock the door. I stick my head out and listen. It's silent. The kind of silence only heard in the winter with snow muffling the usual music of the night.

Closing the door quietly behind me, I venture onto the porch. My feet stop at the edge of the top step. For half a second, I debate leaving it until morning, but I'm already outside. My breath comes out in white plumes before dissipating into the night.

The night is clear and bright. Now that I'm outside, I can see stars glitter faintly across the sky. If not for the light pollution of the moon, it would be perfect for viewing constellations, if I knew what any were besides the big dipper. I rub my arms against the cold. Maybe I will learn more this summer.

I go down the four steps and walk around to the side of the house. Just as I thought, a beat-up old metal trash can has been knocked over. There aren't any bear tracks in the snow, so I take that as a good sign as I straighten it back up.

I turn to go back inside when I see a footprint in the snow just off to my right, somewhere I hadn't stepped, and much too large to be mine even if I had. My heart crashes against my chest.

The faint smell of cigar smoke wafts past me.

Someone's arm snakes around my waist. I open my mouth to scream, but a hand clasps a cloth around my mouth and nose. It smells like chemicals and is sickly sweet. It makes me want to gag. And then I feel my body go limp as I am swallowed up by darkness.

CHAPTER 15

y head is splitting as if someone tried to cleave it in two with a large rock. Every muscle hurts, and I am freezing, not yet numb. It's only a relief because I know it means I haven't been outside long. I try to move into a more comfortable position, but I can't. My body won't move. My eyes fly open, and I am staring at the starry sky, a rounded clearing with large trees framing the edges of my vision. A light dusting of snow is drifting down.

I pull on my arms, and for a second, I think I am paralyzed. But when I drop my head to the side, I see my wrist and ankles are tied by rope, and I am on a large, flat rock.

"W-what?" I jerk on the ties. *How did I get here?* There's the eerie familiarity from my dream again, only this time it is real.

Snow crunches near my other side, but I can't see who it is. I don't know if I should pretend to be unconscious still and hope whoever it is hasn't seen me move or heard me, or . . . All thoughts leave my head when the man comes into view.

He pulls in a large lungful of smoke from the cigar he's smoking and exhales slowly before flicking it to the ground, where it extinguishes in the snow with a hiss. He's the old man from Burger Bar. Only, as impossible as it seems, he can't be much older than thirty.

I realize now how stupid I was to go outside tonight. The ultimate in stupid. It was first-person-to-die-in-a-horror-movie-because-the-dumb-girl-ran-up-the-stairs-instead-of-out-the-open-front-door level of stupid. I literally out-stupided the entire planet.

"Who are you?" I demand. Though, even as I say the words, I think I know exactly who he is.

The neutral expression on his face twists up into a sneer, which is thankfully somehow less creepy than the blank veneer he wore seconds before. He stalks closer to me until he stands at my head, and I have to straighten my neck to look up at him.

"Let me go!"

He leans over, his face only inches from mine. I try to scoot away, but the rope tying me down to this cold boulder prevents me from moving. "What's the matter, Clarke? Don't you recognize me?"

I tug hard on the binds at my wrist. The harsh rope twists against my skin until it's raw.

"What do you want?" There's a tremor in my voice now that I wish I could blame on the cold, but I know it's from fear, because I went numb the second I saw him.

"Happy birthday, Clarke," he says darkly. I hate the way he says my name.

And from the gleam in his eye, he knows it, too.

"I don't care who you are, let me go!" I was wrong. I preferred the creepy doll face. Now he is angry, and I swear red sparks just flickered in his eyes.

"This is exactly why we are here." He trails a hand up my arm, across my shoulder, and over my head then down the other side.

His touch makes me want to retch. I don't know what he's going to do to me, but I know it's worse than anything I could imagine. I inhale a breath to scream, but he is gripping my chin hard enough to leave a bruise. The inside of my mouth is pinched hard against the sharp edges of my teeth until I can taste copper.

"Don't even think about it." He lets go with a painful shove. The back of my head scrapes against the rough-hewn stone. He paces from my head to my feet and back again, stopping once to look at the moon cresting over the trees, making its way directly above us. "Most people call me Tamsin," he says, pressing his hand to his chest as if we were having a formal meeting. "But you, my dear, may call me *Uncle*."

I can barely catch my breath, and it feels like I've been running for miles. "W-where is Michelle?" I ask.

He smiles, and it feels like a thousand spiders are crawling all over my skin, making my nearly frozen muscles clench painfully.

"They thought they could keep you from me," he continues, as if I hadn't spoken at all. "But we are family, and I'm not about to let them keep me from what rightfully belongs to me."

"I don't belong to you, or anyone!"

He laughs. "I am talking about your magic, girl. *That* does belong to me."

I am insulted and angry and scared beyond what I thought possible, though I glare like I am not. His thought process is insane, and completely stupid.

My skin is burning from the cold now. I continue to strain against my ties, but the ropes are too thick and refuse to give even an inch of slack. Pain like pins and needles stabs along the skin of my exposed arms. My jacket is gone, and so are my boots.

"You shouldn't have even been able to get into town," I spit out.

He huffs, then leans his side against the stone and looks down at me. "And why on earth would you think that? You know residents can come and go as they please. The real trick was how I found ways to use magic that wouldn't alert the Court of the Sun and the Moon to what I was doing. The last thing I needed was their interference."

Keep him talking, I tell myself. *Keep him talking. Michelle will find me*. "What do you mean?"

"I mean that I couldn't outright attack you, so I had to get creative. A harmless cloaking spell, a touch of telekinesis . . ." He waves a hand in a circle. "It was all so troublesome. I would have preferred to use magic outright. Of course, that mutt who's been sniffing around found a way to ruin all my attempts and save you like he was your personal knight in shining armor."

Save me? Then it hits me with a hard kick of clarity. The car I didn't see, the incident with the icicles . . . those accidents I had were *not* accidents. My heart speeds up.

"Why am I tied up?" I try to keep him talking. I would rather freeze to death than endure whatever sick plans he has in store for me. I hope Michelle can find me in time, or—

I could kick myself for sending Seth away. He would have kept me from going outside like an idiot. Maybe he could have helped stop this from happening in the first place. And I hate that. I despise that I've put myself in a position to be helpless and in need of rescuing.

"You have your father to thank for that."

I don't know what he's talking about. "My father? He left before I was born. I've never even met him. I have nothing to do with him!"

Whatever worry I had for my dad dissipates and is replaced by anger. Whatever he did to this psycho before I was born, I am being held accountable now. Hate like this couldn't possibly come from something so stupid as not being born as powerful. Then, I remember —Michelle said they'd fought, and Mason hadn't been seen since then.

Tamsin laughs as if I've said something funny, then he disappears out of my line of sight. I strain my neck, trying to see where he went, but the rock prevents me from moving too much.

Something vibrates against my leg, and I nearly jump out of my skin until I realize what it is. My cell. I pull on my arms, and twist my hip toward my hand, slowly, trying to keep my movements as small as I can. Trying to reach my phone, my fingers brush against the material of my pants, but I can't get my hip close enough to reach in and grab it.

I freeze when Tamsin walks into view again. This time, he's holding a painting—*the* painting from the hall at Michelle's. Why would he bring it out here? I glance from his face to the painting and back, and he's looking at me like I should know what it means.

Tamsin pushes it closer to my face when I don't say anything. Two figures stand in the woods . . . *two*. Much closer than before. One that looks exactly like Michelle and the other like the man in front of me, only younger . . . kinder.

My stomach gutters out, and I finally understand.
My dad *didn't* leave. He'd been trapped by his brother.

CHAPTER 16

Tamsin tosses the painting over his shoulder, and my heart skips a beat as I hear a sound I can't identify. I don't know if it ripped or landed paint down in the snow. I hope it's not damaged, because I don't know what would happen to Michelle or my dad if it was ruined.

He looks up at the moon, now almost directly overhead.

"It is nearly time!" he announces with childlike glee.

I don't like the sound of that. "Time for what?"

Tamsin drops his chin to look at me with disgusted disbelief. He sighs in exasperation, folding his arms and rubbing his forehead as if I'm an idiot for not knowing his plan. "For your powers to come in. Didn't they teach you anything? You will be the most powerful—"

"That's stupid." I snort. I take pleasure in the shocked, almost hurt expression he gives me. "There's no way—"

Like a flash of lightning, his arm soars through the air, striking my cheek with the back of his hand. I see stars, and a metallic taste touches my tongue. I can feel the inside of my cheek swell from being cut on my teeth.

"Do you see that bracelet?" He runs a finger over my wrist. "It isn't just a tracking device. It also monitored your powers as they started to emerge, so I know *exactly* how powerful you could be. And once all that power is mine, I can finally be rid of *them* once and for all." He throws a glance over his shoulder toward the discarded painting.

Tracking device . . . so that's how he'd found me, how he managed to be in the same places I'd been. I thought Mom had put it in my bag as an early present. But if my dream was really a memory then when he flipped our car that night, Tamsin would have had the perfect opportunity to plant it in my things. He had known where I was all along.

Tamsin lifts his arm and checks his watch. "It is time to begin."

My phone vibrates against my leg again.

"You don't have to do this!" I nearly shout. "I didn't even know you existed until yesterday."

"That is most unfortunate," he says, but his tone says he couldn't care less.

"Look," I try to reason with him, slow him down until I can get my phone. "If I'd known, I would have looked for you. They tried to keep me in the dark." I take a stab at telling him what I think he might want to hear. "I don't know why you're all fighting, but—"

"Don't lie to me," he bites out. For a second, I think he'll hit me again. He certainly looks like he wants to. Instead, he picks up an old leather-bound book at his feet.

I stretch until I think my left arm will rip from its socket. Finally, I manage to get my right index finger into my pocket and begin swiping at my phone, hoping that somehow I'll be able to reach Seth. I'm so focused on trying to hit the right spots on the screen that I think will send him a message, I don't see Tamsin has noticed me until it's too late.

The book slams shut.

"What are you doing?" He reaches over and grabs my wrist, twisting it in his vise-like grip. I cry out. His icy hand reaches into my pocket and rips my cell out. He throws it to the ground with a loud crack. Then I hear his boot stomp down on it with a crunch. Once. Twice. "We'll not have any of that now."

I go limp. Defeated. Pretty sure this man is going to kill me and there's nothing I can do, nothing anyone can do, because the only people who know where I am are stuck in a painting, and my only hope of getting help is now in a shattered and broken heap on the ground.

Tamsin cracks open the book, the cold leather binding groaning in response. He places it down on the stone slab, and when he raises his hands, he's holding a long knife with a slightly rounded blade.

I panic, afraid he's going to drive it into my chest right here and now. The adrenaline makes it hard to draw in a breath to scream.

Moonlight glints off the sharp point. He plunges the knife down, and I stare in horror as it penetrates his own palm. With a quick jerk, he rips it from his flesh without the slightest hint that he even felt it. The knife clatters to the stone top, forgotten, yet out of my reach.

Tamsin stalks toward me. My screams come out as nothing more than whimpers. He dips the fingers of his other hand into his wound and then grabs my chin painfully as he smears his blood across my forehead, drawing symbols. My teeth cut into the already wounded side of my cheek. The warm sticky feel of his ichor makes me gag.

"Gross," I manage to say. I take pleasure in the look of disdain he's giving me, as if *I* am the one being unreasonable and completely nuts.

He picks up the knife again with his wounded palm. Crimson drips off his hand. I feel like an experiment for a mad scientist. Tamsin tugs on the end of my tee and slices, shredding a piece off and wrapping it around his hand.

Then, in a move I didn't anticipate, Tamsin cuts the rope holding my left hand, and for a second, I think sense has returned to him, but then I scream as he slices my palm through with the knife.

I scream again as he jerks the blade away. He picks up the book again and starts to read.

Strange words make my vision vibrate. And even with one free arm, I am unable to move. My mind buzzes with the maddening noise like a swarm of wasps. The sound scrapes my bones.

Black smoke forms above me and settles on my chest as if it has a consciousness. My breath is controlled by the dark thing sitting on me, and I swear it's a demon. I can feel it reach its rotting hand right through me.

The pain is too much, and I feel my magic for the first time. I feel it awaken and wind its way up, pulled forcefully from its sleeping depths until I gasp from the overwhelming pressure of it.

My eyes roll back. I think this is it. He is going to take my magic like he wanted to take my father's, and he will kill me to possess it.

My thoughts fade into shadows, and I feel everything about who I am start to disappear. I think I hear the song of a wolf crying somewhere far in the distance, but that is soon overpowered by the sharp and ugly words dripping from my uncle's mouth. The intense scent of copper—*the scent of blood*—fills my nose. . . my mouth, and I am drowning in it.

CHAPTER 17

I gasp with the sudden cessation of Tamsin's words as the dark power vanishes in a puff of smoke. My own magic snaps back like a rubber band, but it is not fully part of me anymore. It's more like fog that hovers around me, and I can feel that it has been injured.

Tamsin cries out as the wolf from my mind materializes out of nowhere, slamming its body into him. It is the wolf from my dream. I try to reach out, but I'm weak, and no sound makes it out of my throat. My hand falls limply onto the rock.

There's a familiar scent. Woodsy. Like fire and wood smoke—and something rich and bittersweet. My vision comes and goes as I watch the wolf. It hunches and grows tall and lean, changing its skin to that of a human.

Seth?

"—won't let you hurt her!"

He's standing in the shadows with his back to me. I can barely make out the top half of his shirtless form. Spots dance before my eyes. I reach out toward him, but he can't see. Then he's gone again, and the wolf is standing in his place.

Slowly I regain some feeling in my body, and I realize the tie on my other hand has slackened. I lift my bloody hand to my forehead to stop the spinning and grimace. *How did Seth find me?* How did he know?

My mind is clear now, but still I don't move. Not yet. Seth is moving, trying to block Tamsin's view of me so I can get loose.

Seth growls, and Tamsin lunges, grabbing the knife before I can get to it. Metal scrapes against stone, kicking up sparks. Seth jumps back from me, leading Tamsin farther away.

"Nooo!" I scream.

But they move too fast for me to see, and all I hear is a deep thunk. Limbs and fur blur with unnatural speed. I roll to my side and loosen the tie around my right wrist until I can slip my hand through. My skin is raw and bloody, but I don't have time to see how much damage has been done. I'm fine. I'm fine as long as I can still move.

I scoot toward my feet, fumbling with the rope. My fingers are numb from the cold, and I can barely get them to do what I need. I claw at the binding. My gaze keeps jumping to the two of them as they continue to fight. Tamsin is slashing at Seth, and he barely leaps out of the way in time.

The ties fall away just as the knife plunges into Seth's shoulder. Or is that his chest? I can't tell from this angle. But Seth falls to the ground. He doesn't change back, his wolf form lying still in the snow-covered ground.

"No!" I scream again, my voice straining, burning my raw throat.

Tamsin pauses and meets my eyes with his.

"No?" The question is soft, as if he's actually considering my request. "You care for this . . . *beast?*" He delivers a swift kick to him. I can hear the sound of his boot connecting to Seth's ribs right before the wolf lets out a whimper.

I lick my chapped lips, and I know my protest has given away too much.

Tamsin stalks toward me. I scoot back until I'm on the edge.

"You would betray your own kind, your own *family*, for that abomination?" He's so close that I think he will grab my bruised face again or hit me. But he doesn't touch me. Instead he leans in close until I can feel his rancid breath brush across my cheek. "Don't worry. I will dispose of it when I am done with you."

He makes no move to tie me back down. Perhaps he can see how weak his magic has already made me. Tamsin picks up the book and turns his back to me. He doesn't think I can get away. Maybe he's right, but I'll still try.

I push my legs to the edge of the rock slab, and it's too much. I can feel my own magic wrap around me. I tilt my head back and watch as the moon hits its perfect zenith.

Time slows, and I feel overly full, like a cup, ready to spill over.

The moon's light grows brighter until it swallows up my entire field of vision. It pulls on me like a tractor beam. The world shifts as inch by inch, my magic clicks into place. Strange and foreign and beautiful and familiar all at once. None of it makes sense, but it feels right.

Then there are those words again. Tamsin's harsh grating voice as he begins to read once more, not caring that I managed to get loose. His dark magic scrapes along my own and scrapes bitterly.

My body is no longer my own as I slide off the slab to the frozen ground covered in white. My power is fending off the black magic spewing from Tamsin, but just barely. I rip the silver bracelet from my wrist, and I feel the bindings that muted my magic break. And it's as if I can finally breathe clearly for the first time.

I try to look for Seth, but my muscles won't move. I am paralyzed again by the warring magics. I manage to catch a glimpse of him from the corner of my eye. He is unmoving on his side, his eyes are closed, and red darkens the snow around him.

My dream has come true, and there is nothing I can do about it. Then I fall, slipping away from my magic as it hangs in the air like something tangible that only I can see. Tamsin has finished reading and sets the book down on the stone.

I don't move. I wait for him to turn his back on me. He grabs the knife, walks over to Seth, and kicks him hard, rolling him over onto his side. Seth grunts, and I am glad he is still alive. If only I could get to him and protect him from my uncle.

Tamsin lifts his hand, hovering the knife over Seth as he straddles him, lifting him just slightly off the ground by his neck.

I use the stone for support and push up to my feet as his arm sails through the air, down toward Seth's heart.

CHAPTER 18

I will my power to come back to me. Demand that it obey. I want to scream at Tamsin to stop, to not touch Seth, but my voice is gone.

Tamsin's arm falls. Once again, time slows, and my heart slows with it. I watch the knife fall closer to Seth's chest.

My magic has listened. It's building up inside me, waiting for my command. I reach out, not knowing how to stop what's about to happen. But my magic knows. And it crests like the wave of a tsunami pouring over the edge, spilling up and out and flying in a blinding streak toward them.

I can hear Tamsin screaming. Then there's a painful snap as my power returns to me, knocking me back as if it were a demolition ball. Then there is only the moon and the stars. I gasp, clawing at my chest as I try to catch my breath. It takes a long moment before my lungs remember how to work.

The ground is biting beneath my hands and legs as I am forced to stay seated; my legs are too weak to stand or even crawl. The cold from the snow, soaking through my clothes, is stinging my skin.

Tamsin falls to the ground next to Seth, quiet. I can't tell if he's dead or not until his hand moves, swatting at something I can't see,

94

swinging across his body again and again, until his movements become frantic and he is hysterical.

Black oily smog rises up, swirling around him, forming a lanky beast with a small body and many arms.

The air wavers like heat rising from asphalt. It makes me feel ill, as if I were swallowing bitter poison. He's screaming now, rolling around on the ground, while dark smoke continues to billow around him.

Then his cries go silent, and the air around him clears.

He's not moving. The beast looks me in the eye and hisses before wrapping itself around Tamsin and disappearing behind a dark plume of black. When the air clears, the thing is gone. And so is Tamsin.

I blink, and a weight is lifted.

There's a loud hissing behind me, the sound of a hot poker slowly doused in water. I spin in place where I'm sitting in the mud and slush. The painting Tamsin tossed to the ground is melting though the snow, and more of the same darkness grows out of it, thick and impenetrable.

Then there's a loud crack from the stone I'd been tied to. The connection between my brain and body jumpstarts, and I can move again. I jump and scramble away. More fissures snake their way through the rock. It crumbles into fine rubble, kicking up a thick mass that swallows everything.

Coughing and rasping come from within the dust cloud. Then the billowing blackness crumbles into a thick, fine dust, and the air clears, exposing two figures. The altar is gone, completely, leaving no trace that it had ever been there.

Michelle is standing at the base of the tree next to a man who looks so much like the one who tried to kill me only minutes ago. But he looks a little younger, clean shaven with evident smile lines.

The man has to be Mason . . . *my dad*. So many thoughts and emotions tumble through me. I've been angry at him for so long for walking out on us. But he didn't.

They spot me, and Michelle rushes to my side, gathering me in her arms, hugging me and kissing the top of my head. She pulls back.

"How did you escape?" I ask.

"When he died, so did his curse and everything his dark magic created," Michelle says. "I knew you could do it."

I still. Was she implying that *I* killed him? I'd only wanted to stop him from hurting Seth. I look back over my shoulder, not nearly as fazed as I would have expected. I mean, nearly being murdered . . . a demon . . . shock. It has to be shock. When it all hits me, it is going to be ugly. I already know that much.

A shudder walks down my spine, echoing through my entire body. Tamsin disappeared. Though Michelle just said he died, I have to know if he'll find some way to come back and get me. I have to know he won't be back for my family.

"Where did he go?"

"He made a deal with a demon, and when he failed to deliver, the demon took him as payment." Michelle explains, angling her body and waving Mason over. He hesitates. "Mason, come meet your daughter."

At that last word, he brightens and rushes to close the distance. He scoops me up, hugging me tight and spinning me in a circle. It should be weird and uncomfortable. But as he crushes me to his chest, I find all those feelings I'd had growing up—being mad at him—melt. He'd been trapped in a piece of art.

My father takes my face in his hands and examines me with a look that's a cross between pride and sorrow. "You've grown so much," is all he says, then he's hugging me again.

"Seth," I say. "He's hurt—" I pull away from my dad and somehow manage to amble over to Seth's side. He's lying on his back, the barrel of his chest heaving. I drop down next to his side, covering my mouth with one hand, stifling a sob and stroking his large wolf head with the other. "I thought he killed you."

Seth lifts his head at my voice and rolls to his belly. I swear he's smiling at me in wolf form. Part of his lip is lifted slightly on one side to reveal an elongated canine. Then he sits up.

I push his big head out of the way and examine the wound. It's much too small an injury for the size of the blade.

"Clarke," Michelle's voice draws me away. "You're shaking— You're not wearing any shoes! We need to get out of here before you lose your toes to frostbite."

"What about Seth?" I protest.

Michelle waves a hand. "He'll be fine. He will heal in a few hours."

"How?" I ask.

Michelle smiles. "There's plenty of time to discuss that when we are somewhere warmer."

Mason picks me up in a sudden sweeping motion. I let out a surprised squeak, and if I didn't know better, I'd say Seth was laughing. I still manage to stick my tongue out at him.

I am exhausted and so cold that everything hurts, but I'm determined to stay as strong as everyone else. To keep from giving in to the sudden lack of strength as the adrenaline leaves my body.

It's a longer walk than I expected, but Seth leads the way, following a set of large footprints. His paws step over them, erasing the last marks Tamsin left behind. A set of two uninterrupted lines trail next to them. I study them for a second only to realize that monster had dragged me through the snow instead of carrying me over his shoulder!

Michelle walks next to us, her hand coming up to stroke my hair every few yards. I don't know where Seth is leading us, but he seems to be sniffing out a trail. After several long minutes, Mom's car comes into view. My eyes widen.

"You drove?" I ask loudly.

Seth cocks his head and snorts. Michelle laughs. I get the feeling I missed something, but I'm pretty sure that whatever Seth implied was wolfy-sarcasm.

"It seems Tamsin wasn't strong enough to use magic to get you all the way out here," Michelle says, answering the question I meant to ask.

"Where exactly are we?"

This time, it's Mason who answers, "We have to be at least twenty-five miles outside of town. Tamsin would have to be outside of the wards to attempt—" He cuts himself off, his grip on me tightening.

We all understand the words he doesn't say.

Michelle opens the car door and slides into the driver's seat. The engine roars to life. And only then does Dad put me down so he can open the back door for me.

I climb in, grateful to have my feet in something other than snow. I reach for the door and stop to look at Seth. "Why haven't you changed back yet?"

"Well, probably because he'll be naked, dear," Michelle says from the front seat.

I can feel heat try to rise up my face at having nearly seen everything earlier. I like him, but it's way too soon for that. "If you pop the trunk, there should be a blanket there."

A minute later, the other door to the back opens, and Seth is standing there, wrapped in nothing but the blanket. His grin spreads wide, and I realize I've been staring.

I look away, and he climbs in next to me. Michelle drives off the path where we'd been parked to the road.

Finally, I look at Seth, making sure to only look him in the eye. "Are you hurt badly?"

"I'm fine. It will be fully healed in a few hours, just like your aunt said—"

He wouldn't tell me if he was bleeding out. I pull the blanket away from his chest to look.

"Are you always so rough?" he asks, wincing.

It's hard to believe, but no one else is worried. "Wha—"

He wiggles his eyebrows, and his smile grows even larger. Finally getting the double entendre, I swat gently at his uninjured shoulder, then shove more blanket at him.

Seth puts his hand on the back of my head and pulls me to him, resting his forehead on mine.

"Thank you for worrying about me," he says quietly. Then he kisses me. His fingers tangle in my hair. He pulls me closer, refusing to let me go until his fear passes completely. I think my lips will bruise, but I can feel his relief that I'm okay. After a moment, the pressure lightens, but he continues to kiss me.

Mason coughs loudly, followed by Michelle shushing him, telling him to let us be.

The cold has filled me down to the marrow of my bones, and I am mostly numb. Slowly, Seth's warmth penetrates my skin, thawing me.

He finally relinquishes my lips, and my mind goes blank. My breath is quick, though truthfully, if I didn't need to breathe, I would still be kissing him.

I look into his amber eyes. I don't know if I believed he was a wolf shifter until I saw him change.

"Did you know the ancient Greeks invented the spiked collar to protect their sheep-herding dogs from wolves?" The words spill past my lips. I can't believe I just said that. I clamp a hand over my mouth, horrified.

"What?" He laughs at me. And then that crooked smile appears on his face again.

I shrug. "I'm sorry. That was rude," I mutter.

He shakes his head and hugs me closer, placing a kiss on my forehead. "You and your random facts." He looks me up and down, no doubt noting how inadequately dressed I am. Soaked flannel pants, bare feet, and a tee. "You're freezing."

My skin is red from the cold.

"I'm fine," I say. Though I think he knows I'm full of it.

He scoffs, then wraps me up in his arms. He's stronger than he should be. It's awkward, but I don't fight it, because he's warm. I wrap my arms around him and nuzzle my face into the crook of his neck. The steady sway of the car along the road and the absence of the stark cold relaxes me.

The car ride is long and silent. I think we are all trying to process the events. Either that, or Michelle and Mason—*Dad*—think I'm sleeping. Regardless, I'll take it.

Seth insists on carrying me from the car to the house, even though I tell him I can walk, and I'm worried the blanket will slip. He only presses me tighter against him, giving in when he can set me down on the couch. I grab his hand, and he turns to go.

I don't want to be alone. Not right now. I want as many people here with me as I can get. The idea of being by myself makes my throat tight.

Seth's hand squeezes mine. "Let me get dressed, and I'll be right back."

"You have clothes here?" I ask.

"When I came to check on you again, I saw the door open. I knew something had happened. I stripped before I shifted." He nods to the pile of discarded clothing on the floor.

I nod, then let go, watching him walk into the other room. He's not gone long, and just seeing that cocky smile eases me. He crosses the room and sits next to me, pulling me into his side.

"I'll get the first aid kit and wrap your hand," Michelle says and walks from the room.

I look down. I'd nearly forgotten about it. Flexing the muscles slightly, I hiss through my teeth. Now it hurts. To get my mind off it until Michelle returns, I look up at Mason. It's weird to think of him as my dad. But that's who he is. He didn't desert us. He was imprisoned. "You were here the whole time?"

He nods, then takes a blanket off the back of one of the chairs and drapes it over me. I worry I'll get it filthy, but quickly dismiss that thought. I'm freezing and happy for the added warmth.

"I tried to get Michelle's attention for years, but she would never look."

"Mason!" Michelle scolds playfully from behind him. He flinches as he laughs. Then her features soften. "I kept it because you made it . . . but looking at it only reminded me that you were missing." He puts an arm around her and gives her a hug, only to be pushed away seconds later. "You smell to high heaven. Go shower."

"You wouldn't smell that great if you were stuck in a painting for eighteen years—"

"Go now. We'll talk more when you're out."

Dad slinks off to the bathroom, looking back at me as if he doesn't want to let me out of his sight.

"You'll have all the time in the world with her." Michelle points toward the bathroom. "Now."

He listens, leaving Michelle to tend to my hand. She sits on the coffee table in front of me. Her fingers move deftly, cleaning and bandaging the cut on my palm. Her eyes flick to Seth a few times, as if she's unsure of him. I know she trusts him, but I think him liking me was not something she'd expected.

"And what about you?" she asks him when she finally relinquishes my hand.

Seth shakes his head.

"Fine." She sighs. "Then I'm going to make some food. I'm sure Mason is starving." She pushes up and heads to the kitchen.

Seth and I are alone now. I turn to him, and before I can utter a word, he grabs my face and kisses me, hard. His tongue grazes my lips, and I lean into him, melting as his fingers brush against my jaw and down my neck.

I groan when he pulls away, not entirely ready for the kiss to end.

"I'm sorry," Seth says.

I list my head to the side and frown. "Why?"

"For not coming sooner."

I shake my head. "How could you have known? I didn't exactly make it easy for you to be here. How *did* you know where to find me?"

"I was in town." He shrugs as if it isn't a big deal. Then, more seriously, he adds, "I was worried when I saw Michelle's car still at the bakery, even though she'd left hours before. I knew something was wrong. Then you wouldn't respond to my calls or texts. I knew you were home." He gives me a frown. Not an angry one, more sweet, like he can't help but pout about it. "I smelled your scent here, but something just didn't feel right. It was different than usual, so I went scouting to see if I could find the source, but he was too far ahead of me. Then I scented you."

"Ohmygawd, what?" I ask, horrified. He can *smell* me? What on earth do I smell like? My face burns from the embarrassment, heat climbing up my chest and neck to my face.

"Your magic, I mean." He laughs as he clarifies. I relax a little. Still not overly thrilled that the guy I like can scent me. This might lead to a complex. "The rest, you know."

"Well, thank you for saving me." I lean back into the cushions of the couch, pinning Seth's arm under me. I don't want him to leave, but I am so tired, I can hardly keep my eyes open.

"I'm just glad you're safe," he murmurs quietly into my hair as he kisses me on the top of my head and wraps an arm around me. "Does this mean you'll let me take you out for your birthday?"

I snort but nod as I mumble something I mean to be a yes but is probably more of an unintelligible noise.

By the time my dad and Michelle rejoin us, I'm too tired to keep my eyes open, so I let the quiet lull of their voices comfort me as I finally let sleep take me.

CHAPTER 19

$\mathcal{I}$ wake to Seth's arm around me. I feel safe. I honestly don't think I could have slept at all if he hadn't been here. I snuggle deeper into his side, pressing my ear tighter against his chest, listening to the steady thump of his heart.

The door opens, and in comes a blast of cold air and flakes of snow fluttering everywhere. My eyes shoot wide open. Every trace of the sleepy peace I had seconds ago has vanished. I rub my bleary eyes, clearing the sleep from them. When the door closes, Mom is standing there, grinning down at me.

It takes several seconds for reality to hit me. Then I'm rolling off the couch and onto the floor as I scramble to my feet and run to her. She wraps her arms around me and squeezes me tight.

"Mom!" I cry. There's not a scratch on her. "I thought you were still too hurt!"

"What is going on out—" I hear Michelle start.

"Angela?" Mason says softly.

Michelle joins our hug, but Mason hangs back. Mom and Michelle are talking at the same time, crying happy tears. I am squished and uncomfortable, but it is still the best feeling in the world.

"Mason," Mom says, finally realizing he's here. The look on her face is a mixture of happiness and pain. She shakes her head. "Why? How?" She motions around the room.

Michelle cuts him off before he gets the chance to speak. "He never left. Tamsin trapped him in the painting. It was never his choice."

Mom sniffs and looks from Mason to the wall where the painting used to hang. Countless feelings I couldn't even begin to guess flitter across her face. Then she says, "You were stuck in that ugly thing this whole time?"

Mason blinks a few times before laughing. Mom runs into his arms, pushing him back a step, and he doesn't hesitate to hold her. "I'm still mad at you."

But I can tell there's no real anger there. It will take time, but I know from her reluctance to let him go that she's already forgiven his absence for the last eighteen years, just as I have. Of course we all have a lot of adjusting to do, but I think the love they have always had for each other will make our family fall into place in no time.

It takes several minutes for everything to quiet down and break apart. We each take a seat, either on the couch or in one of the plush chairs, and talk. I tell Mom about everything that happened with Tamsin in the woods, with Mason and Michelle, and even Seth, adding details here and there.

"How are you out of the hospital?" I ask again.

Mom nods and gives me a tight-lipped smile. "After the car crashed on the way to Havenwood Falls, I knew Tamsin had found us. I was hoping we'd be able to make it to the safety of the wards before he could reach us. But before I could do anything, he struck. He poisoned me with his magic. I was conscious the whole time, but I was unable to move." Mom's voice hitches. She looks up in Michelle's direction then back to me. "I'm just glad your aunt brought us to Havenwood Falls. I tried fighting the effects of his magic, but I'm not very strong." She drops her chin and looks down at her hands for a long moment before balling them into a fist. "I shouldn't have shut out my magic like I did when I was younger. If I'd learned how to control it better, I might have been able to wake up earlier, and you might never have been taken." She cups my cheek and meets my gaze, her own eyes filling with tears. "I'm so sorry, Clarke. But as soon as he died, his magic died too, and I was able to wake up."

"I'm sorry, but . . . what?" It wasn't that what she was saying didn't make sense. I remember the sharp smell of copper and realize now it was Tamsin's magic I'd sensed that day. I shudder, realizing how clueless I was, . . . how close I was to losing her to that monster. "It might have helped to know about him and magic and everything else before we moved here," I say, picking at my nails. I'm not mad. I know Mom did what she felt was best.

"Oh, Michelle, really!" Mom scolds gently. "You didn't tell her anything?"

"I told her some of it, but in my defense, you did tell me that you wanted to do this together." Michelle averts her gaze. "I had no idea Tamsin was so close."

Mom puts a hand on her leg and gives her a comforting squeeze. "It's okay. It's really my fault. I should have thought everything through. I was just so worried, I couldn't think straight." Then she turns to me once more. "Our powers are at their strongest when the moon is full, but are also most vulnerable when they first come in. That is why your uncle needed to try to steal your powers last night. He was at his strongest, and you, your most vulnerable."

I already knew about the moon thing, because Michelle explained that. But . . . "Would he have killed me?" I ask.

She nods solemnly. Then, after a moment's hesitation, she leans forward and hugs me. It must be hard for her to admit it, but I appreciate her candor. "We will start training you as soon as you're ready."

I frown at this. I'd struck Tamsin when I'd meant to. My magic had known what I wanted. I assumed this is how it works. "What do you mean? Don't I already know how to use my magic?"

I move back to the couch, to Seth's side. The warmth radiating from him is soothing.

"You do at the most basic level. I believe it worked as well as it did on Tamsin because of the moon's position and because your will was so strong in that moment." Mom looks back over her shoulder at Michelle and Mason. "You're powerful, the most powerful Price in generations, but without training, there is a chance your magic could turn dark."

That thought is terrifying. My hands grow ice cold and clammy. If a lack of training equals power possibly going to the dark side of things, then . . .

"You said Tamsin wasn't very powerful," I accuse my aunt.

She looks down. "He wasn't. But it was his heart that twisted his magic." They all have that look that says there is way more to this than they are saying. "We worry, because his dark magic touched you. He was partway through the ritual, which opened your magic up to his darkness."

"Oh," I say. "Why didn't anyone tell me about any of this before?" I blurt out, hurt that so much was kept from me. Mom should have told me everything years ago. At the very least, she should have told me when we left to move here.

Mom opens her arms and motions for me to come to her. And I do, because I'm relieved that she's okay. That she has been this entire time.

"I'm sorry, sweetie. We didn't tell you because we thought that the less you knew, the safer you'd be."

I lean back, scrunch up my face at her, and say, "That's stupid logic." Then I pull back. "We?" I look to Michelle, but she's avoiding my eyes and looking at Mason.

Mom laughs. "I thought if you knew about it, then you'd be tempted to experiment with your magic and draw attention to yourself. I didn't want your uncle to find you."

Seth has been quiet the entire time. Nothing about his expression tells me any of this surprises him or is in any way new to him. If it is, he's doing an excellent job of hiding it. I rub my hands over my face and wince from the pain in my palm. "Just promise me one thing— from now on, if there's anything I need to know, please tell me. Don't try to hide it to 'save' me."

They all agree without a fight. That was much easier than I

expected. I let her go and lean back into Seth's side. Everyone looks relaxed and happy . . .

Except for Mason. He's fidgeting with his hands in a way that doesn't fit his stature and looking at Mom like she is the sun and the moon, like she is his entire world. He drops to one knee and pulls out a small box from the pocket of his slacks.

"I was going to propose to you the next day. I carried this stupid thing around in my pocket for a month before, just wondering if we were too young." Mason looks at me and smiles before focusing on Mom again. "I wasted time then, and I don't want to spend another minute without you as my wife." He pulls back the lid to reveal a thin gold band with a single diamond on top and a simple white gold flourish. "Angela, will you—"

"Oh, get up, Mason!" Mom says. Her cheeks grow a bit pink. "We have a lot to talk about before we get to anything of the sort." Sheepishly, Dad stands and puts the ring away. Mom swats at him, missing. "There's plenty of time for that."

Then he laughs. It's not the response I expected. He runs a hand through his hair. "You're right. It's hard to remember that even though it only feels like a few months for me, it's been nearly two decades for you." He gives a slight shake of his head. "Time moved differently in there."

Mom hugs him tight, then plants a big kiss on his mouth. I look away. That was borderline embarrassing, but I see why they were together. They're both slow to anger and have a lighthearted view on the world. It might not be today, or tomorrow, or even next week, but our family is becoming whole.

I bite my lip. I've never seen her so happy before. Group hugs and happy tears commence once again, though not nearly as crushing.

Michelle manages to disengage, and I follow suit, letting my parents have their moment. Seth stands for the first time and wraps an arm around my shoulders.

It has always been just me and Mom. It's so overwhelming now, but in the best possible way. I have a father and an aunt. I never expected I'd have a family. Not like this. But I do, and I would do everything again a thousand times over to keep it.

Mom and Mason—*Dad*—pull apart just slightly, and each hold out one arm to me. I rush to their side and hug them again for possibly the hundredth time since Mom walked through that door.

And everything finally feels complete.

We hope you enjoyed this story in the Havenwood Falls High series of novellas featuring a variety of supernatural creatures. The series is a collaborative effort by multiple authors. Each book is generally a stand-alone, so you can read them in any order, although some authors will be writing sequels to their own stories. Please be aware when you choose your next read.

Other books in the Young Adult Havenwood Falls High series:

Cast in Moonlight by Ali Winters
Promise the Moon by Kallie Ross
Blurred Lines by Daniele Lanzarotta (May 2019)
Ascending Darkness by J.L. Weil (June 2019)

More books releasing on a monthly basis. Stay up to date at www.
HavenwoodFalls.com

Subscribe to our reader group and receive free stories and more!

ABOUT THE AUTHOR

Ali Winters is a USA Today bestselling author as well as an Amazon and international bestselling author. She was born and raised in the Pacific Northwest, where she developed her love of nature, animals, and all things green.

For as long as she can remember, she's been mesmerized by the extraordinary world of books and fantasy. There has never been a time when stories were not begging to be told, either by drawing, photography, or writing.

With encouragement from one of her favorite authors, she jumped in, head first, to pursue the career that had been calling to her since the day she opened her first book.

She has a deep love for coffee, tea, warm blankets, dogs, creating art in any medium she can get her hands on, and family.

Connect with Ali online at
www.aliwinters.com
www.facebook.com/authoraliwinters
www.instagram.com/authoraliwinters
www.twitter.com/aliwinters_
www.bookbub.com/authors/ali-winters

ACKNOWLEDGMENTS

Ever since I discovered the small town of Havenwood Falls, I've wanted to be part of the family. I want to thank Kristie Cook, the creator of this magical and amazing little town, for welcoming me into the Havenwood Falls family. It has been a *blast* to write alongside the others. This has been a wonderful challenge that has allowed me to grow and stretch my wings.

Thank you to Michelle Fritz for your constant support and friendship. For letting me come to you with questions, ideas, and feedback. I hope you love your namesake in the story.

And lastly, to the readers. Authors would be nowhere without you —I would be nowhere without you. You mean the world to me. Thank you for joining me on this journey to Havenwood Falls.

AN EXCERPT

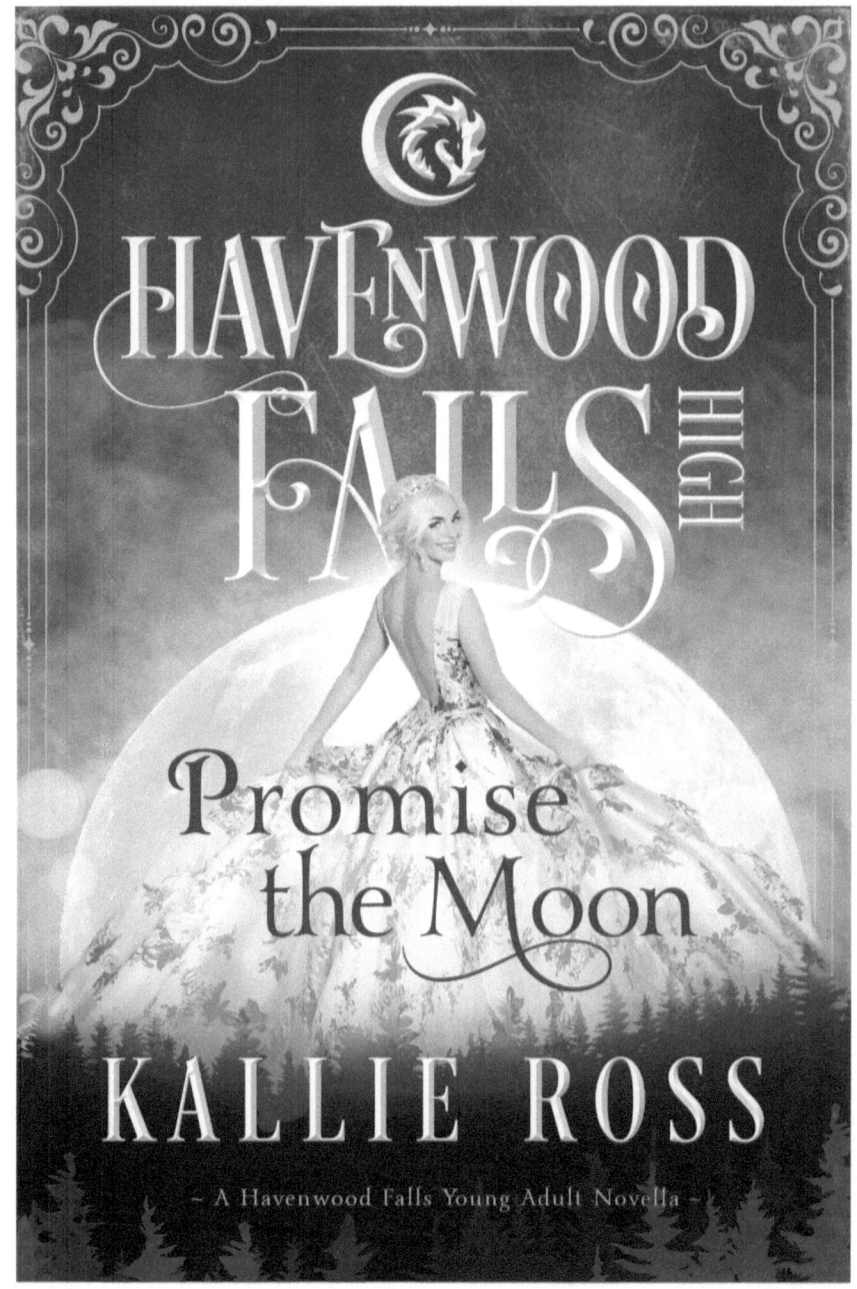

HAVENWOOD FALLS HIGH

Promise the Moon

KALLIE ROSS

~ A Havenwood Falls Young Adult Novella ~

Promise the Moon (A Havenwood Falls High Novella) by Kallie Ross

With her future already fated by others, vampire-hybrid Elle makes the most of her present—but a friend's betrayal could end it all.

Seventeen-year-old vampire-dryad hybrid Elle can't live up to her parents' expectations. She's snubbed by her dad's bloodline-obsessed vampire family while her mom's dryad side has determined her fate—to return to New York City and protect Central Park.

Unsure of her place in the world yet held to promises her family made, Elle dreads leaving her friends as well as breaking things off with her wolf-shifter boyfriend, Kase. With her destiny out of her hands, Elle is determined to control what she can.

Even though Kase Kasun has spent his life living in the shadows of his family name and the weight it carries, he's embraced his role as a protector of Havenwood Falls. Everything had been worked out, until Elle started distancing herself. Kase knows the space she's creating between them will only make room for trouble.

Intent on savoring every last minute together, Elle, Kase, and all their friends plan an epic Spring Break camping trip. But when one of Elle's so-called friends turns out to be an enemy intent on taking her out of Havenwood Falls, her life may come to an untimely end. Promises are made to be broken, and only the moon has the power to save her now.

PROMISE THE MOON

KALLIE ROSS

The Havenwood Falls High bell rang sharply, alerting me to the end of the school day. Finally, spring break. Lifting my head from the pages of my assigned reading, *A Tale of Two Cities,* I watched the rest of the class hustle toward the hallway. Normally, I loved losing myself in a good book, but even with two years of French, I had a hard time keeping up with Darnay and the Defarges.

The thick novel didn't fit in my backpack, so I secured the tattered paperback in my coat pocket, shouldered my bag, and made my way to my locker. There was no need to carry thirty pounds of books, since I'd only need one of them to complete my homework. The weight didn't bother me, because I had super strength. Being a vampire half-breed had perks; for example, I didn't have to deal with bloodlust like my father did. Dryad blood pumped through my veins, powerful enough to subdue any unbecoming urges a young vampire would have. Only problem was each half-breed benefit came with inconveniences, like being able to hear every thought from every mind in the building. Over the last year, with the help of my parents, friends, and night classes at the Academy, I'd mostly learned to control each of my abilities, including the ones I hadn't expected.

The school's hallways always buzzed with the latest gossip and hormones. Tuning out self-conscious teenagers had become second nature. Disregarding arrogant and even lustful thoughts took a little more concentration. And the weirdest part of mind reading wasn't all the jumbled thoughts, but it was seeing them in my mind's eye. My ability was similar to reading a book and visualizing the story like a movie.

So when I heard Ana Novak's thoughts about Kase Kasun, I not only caught a few details about what a good kisser he was, but I envisioned Kase's lips so close I could feel his warm breath brush over my cheek.

I pressed my palm to my forehead to clear my thoughts.

When I looked up, the two were at the end of the corridor across from my locker. Ana was leaning against the old blue-painted metal facing Kase, and she grinned up at him and giggled. Then, as if she sensed I was watching, she nudged his shoulder playfully. Her touch lingered a second too long. He glanced down at the spot she'd touched and shook his head. Her bottom lip pouted out flirtatiously, and he ignored her attempt to win him back and turned to walk in my direction without a word.

As his eyes met mine, he frowned. We'd both been trying to ignore the spectacle Ana made of herself on a daily basis, but somehow she'd found out I called things off romantically with Kase during the holiday break. Ever since, I'd been trying to avoid both of them. Kase had known from the beginning, since his split with Ana, that I wasn't staying. My family had always expected me to move back to New York after graduation. Not to mention, I'd die if I didn't bond with a tree in Central Park by my next birthday. After I'd gained control of my strange powers, and the rumors about the mysterious death of my ex-boyfriend were replaced by who wore what at the latest gala, I'd had to beg my parents to allow me to stay in Havenwood Falls to graduate. Neither of my parents were biological, but they'd been looking after me since the night they found me. I'd been no more than a few months old, and I'd been laid at the foot of my mother's tree in the park.

Kase and I had agreed to stay friends after the holidays, but seeing him through Ana's thoughts made me want to vomit. Every day, the love I felt for Kase grew heavier in my chest. For the last few months, when I knew he had a class in one hallway, I'd go down another so I wouldn't have to face him. Lugging love around, instead of giving it to Kase, made me realize sadness isn't a void. True sorrow is a weight.

Behind him, Ana gave me a death glare. I shrugged and turned toward the exit. Avoiding Ana had become essential for both of us. She had a way of making me crazy, and I couldn't risk losing control in a school filled with humans who didn't know about our supernatural world.

Thirty pounds wasn't that heavy anyway.

Kase walked faster to catch up with me, and I could feel him getting closer. Eluding him had been impossible. The warmth he radiated had to be because he was a wolf shifter; at least, that's what I'd convinced myself. It couldn't be anything more. We couldn't be anything more than friends. It would be easier the next time I saw him. The truth was I'd be seeing him more this next week than I'd allowed myself for months.

Kase cleared his throat, and when I looked over at him, one corner of his mouth pulled up, revealing a dimple.

"You have mean girl cooties," I teased, and wrinkled my nose when he tried to hold my hand—again. It was partially my fault he kept trying. The few times we found ourselves alone, usually because I'd been hanging out with his sister, I felt drawn to him. He had to feel it, too.

When Kase frowned, disappointed at my rejection, my heart ached.

Kase Kasun was everything I'd wanted in a guy when I was wishing for the perfect boyfriend in middle school. Back then, I was just a normal girl, my powers hadn't been triggered, and I'd attended an all-girls prep school in New York City. There was something dreamy about ending up with the All-American athletic good guy. Only, this good guy had gotten himself caught in the claws of an evil, power-hungry she-wolf before I'd arrived.

Kase's steps synced with mine, the rhythm echoing slightly in the emptying hall, and he reached in front of me to open the door leading to the parking lot. My backpack brushed against his forearm. In an effort to avoid knocking him over, I shifted the weight and nearly tipped myself over from being so top heavy. Kase used his wolf-like reflexes to catch me.

I stiffened in his arms.

"Come on, Elle," Kase whispered, and I melted. His olive skin was smooth and his dark eyes warm and inviting. Kase had been the star quarterback of our high school's football team the last two years, and there was no mistaking the muscular build under his letterman's jacket.

He brushed some of my long blond hair over my shoulder to get a better look at my face. He'd discovered all of my tells while we dated, and I could feel him analyzing me. Forcing myself to remain indifferent, I relaxed my jaw, released the inside of my cheek from between my teeth, and loosened my grip on the straps of my backpack.

"How about I take you out for coffee?" he asked. The simplicity of his invitation didn't imply anything more.

I gave him a tight smile, determined to stay strong and let him down easy. "I could use one, but you know I have training."

"Will you stay with me? Please. Even if it's only for a few minutes." Kase's voice croaked, and he gently pulled me a little closer. "We can just talk out here. I miss being with you."

My body betrayed me and leaned into him. Why couldn't we sit at Coffee Haven all afternoon and hang out with our friends? I thought after pushing Kase away for so long, it would be easier to turn him down. Last month, on Valentine's Day, I'd stayed home and claimed to be sick, all in an effort to keep Kase out of sight and out of mind.

My wall was crumbling.

"How about we get that coffee," I agreed with some hesitation, and quickly scrambled to rebuild my façade. "But as friends."

Kase slowly released me, careful to make sure I had my balance.

"I'll take what I can get." His mouth formed a tight smile, and he waved a hand in front of himself, allowing me to lead the way.

Our cars were parked side by side at the back of the lot. His blue truck made my black smart car look like a toy. He and his twin sister,

Willa, shared the truck, but Willa always had archery practice after school. Her boyfriend, Tarron, also on the team, always gave her a ride home.

"Wanna ride together?" Kase asked and chuckled as he looked from his truck to the car. "I'll even try to squeeze into your car if you want to drive. Maybe you can open the sunroof so I can sit up straight."

Before I could stop myself, my hand flung out and backhanded his chest. Kase was over six feet tall, and while I was considered average height, he still towered over me. He'd always teased me about my car, and it almost felt normal to joke about it. Only, our normal had been being *together*, and we would have to figure out a new normal. My goal the past few months had been to avoid running into him altogether. Since his sister was one of my best friends, it proved more difficult than I'd anticipated.

"Haha." My fake laughter was filled with a good dose of sarcasm, and I rolled my eyes as I rummaged through the front pocket of my backpack for my keys. Kase moved around my car to open the driver's side door, and I pushed one of the buttons on my key fob as he rounded the front.

A loud honk blared, making him jump, and I couldn't contain my real laughter. The surprise on his face morphed into a genuine grin.

"That's what you get." My chest filled with warmth, even though it was freezing outside. Being with Kase made me happy, so why couldn't we ride to Coffee Haven together without it being *together?* My lips twisted as I thought, and I made my decision.

"Let's just take your truck," I said and reached for the handle of the passenger door. Kase beat me to it, and opened the door for me. Always the gentleman, he took my backpack and tossed it into the back. Pulling *A Tale of Two Cities* out of my coat pocket, I set it in the middle of the bench seat. Kase climbed into the driver seat and looked down at the novel, with its dog-eared pages and worn cover.

"Is that one for class or for fun?" he asked as he started the truck.

The novel was not what I'd call fun, but Kase was really trying. His friendship would be the one I'd miss most when I moved back to New York.

"Definitely class," I answered. "It's been too long since I've read a book for fun."

Kase put his truck into reverse and backed out of the space. He'd started to put his arm along the back of the seat when he looked behind to check for other cars, but stopped himself. He sounded easygoing, but his posture was rigid, and he almost seemed nervous. After maneuvering out of the parking lot, he relaxed a little.

"So what have you been doing for fun?" he asked softly, keeping his eyes on the road.

When I shifted to face him, the seatbelt threatened to decapitate me. Wrapping my hand around the stiff fabric, I pulled it under my arm and answered, "Mostly training and hanging out with Scarlet and your sister. My parents are still back and forth to New York on business. I almost think they feel bad about being gone so much. Last week, my dad brought a telescope home and said I needed a hobby."

"Soon you'll have track and field season to keep you busy," Kase said, and he shrugged sheepishly. "But until then, astronomy sounds cool."

"Yeah, I guess," I agreed half-heartedly.

"No, really, the sky can tell you so much, especially at night. Knowing the phases of the moon and the different constellations can help you navigate by the stars. You can even tell time by connecting Polaris to the Big Dipper."

Squinting at Kase, I wondered who the imposter was, and asked, "Who are you, and what have you done with Kase?"

He smiled and rubbed at the back of his neck with one hand. "It's me, I promise. There's a lot more that goes into patrolling the town borders than racing against Joe from one ridge to the other. And, in the state he's in, we haven't done much racing. It's not like I have to worry about the phases of the moon because I can control when I shift, but I've had to use the constellations a time or two to stay on course. And I've used the moon to help tell time. Did you know the moon has no light of its own? It's how the sun shines on it that makes it useful."

"That's cool," I said and placed a finger on my chin thoughtfully. "Maybe I'll actually tilt the telescope up and take a look."

"Tilt it up, huh?" he asked with a mischievous grin.

"You may patrol the borders, but somebody has to keep an eye out for the people in town." A giggle escaped me.

Kase slowed the truck down as we approached the four-way stop at Main and Eighth Streets. He looked over at me and asked, "And who exactly do you feel like you need to keep an eye out for?"

"Oh, no one in particular. Think of it as a neighborhood watch," I said with a smirk.

"Sounds more like stalking to me," he mumbled with a chuckle. The truck moved through the intersection, and Kase was on the lookout for a parking space.

"I don't like your tone." So I decided to flip the script. "What have you been doing for fun?"

Kase pulled into a space across the street from Coffee Haven. He kept the truck running, with the heat on, and unbuckled his seatbelt. "Hanging out with Joe mostly. He's missing Infiniti. It's kind of making him crazy. I know you're going to find this cheesy, but kind of like the moon needs the sun to be useful, I've discovered I don't have much fun without you in my life."

Shifting in my seat, I faced forward. He'd gone there. My head pressed back into the seat, and I sighed.

"I can't—no, I won't let you talk me into *this*." I waved my pointer finger between us back and forth a few times. Pausing to gauge where his mind was at, I heard nothing. Kase had blocked me. He'd learned to veil his thoughts from me by the end of our second date.

"I know you're trying to protect me—" he started.

"Don't think I'm some saint. I'm also trying to protecting me." My hand covered my heart.

"I promise to never hurt you." Kase scooted closer, and the paperback between us pressed against my thigh. He lifted his hand and cupped my jawline.

Leaning into him, I closed my eyes and whispered, "That's like promising me the moon, Kase. It kills me to see you every day in those hallways, and a few weeks ago I even stayed away, thinking it might be a little easier. But not seeing you was worse. I thought a half vampire, half dryad dating a wolf shifter was trite, but the fact that I don't know how I'm going to live in New York without you feels pathetic."

"You are anything but pathetic," Kase muttered, his warm breath caressing my cheek. "Elliot Martin, the only I question I have for you is are you doing all of this—keeping me in the friend zone, moving back to New York—for you or for your parents?"

Pulling away, I felt weak. He was the only person in town I'd ever explained my past to, and he was partially right. I wanted to press my lips against his more than anything. Even though I'd been training for over a year to build my strength, to learn to control my power, I was completely vulnerable when it came to Kase.

So I reached for the handle and opened my door. The ice-cold air flooded the cab of the truck. When Kase pulled back in shock, I turned and retreated across the street and into Coffee Haven.

Purchase *Promise the Moon* where books are sold.

www.ingramcontent.com/pod-product-compliance
Lightning Source LLC
Chambersburg PA
CBHW020404130626
46549CB00006B/2438